<u>Also By Marco Conelli</u>

Matthew Livingston and the Prison of Souls

Matthew Livingston and the Millionaire Murder

Matthew Livingston and the Politics of Death

Matthew Livingston Mystery Series #3

MARCO CONELLI

iUniverse, Inc.
New York   Bloomington

Matthew Livingston and the Politics of Death
Matthew Livingston Mystery Series #3

iUniverse books may be ordered through booksellers or by contacting:

iUniverse
1663 Liberty Drive
Bloomington, IN 47403
www.iuniverse.com
1-800-Authors (1-800-288-4677)

ISBN: 978-1-4502-6628-4 (pbk)
ISBN: 978-1-4502-6629-1 (cloth)
ISBN: 978-1-4502-6630-7 (ebk)

Printed in the United States of America

iUniverse rev. date: 10/18/2010

CHAPTER 1

Miserable!

That was my initial reaction. In fact, I didn't think there were enough adjectives in my school's English curriculum to describe how bad this assignment was going to be. As an aspiring journalist, I could not think of a more suitable word.

It was *that* bad!

Believe me; optimism was fueling my fire this particular morning when I arrived at school. Every other Monday I report to Mr. C's classroom on the first floor. This is where I discover what my latest writing stint will be. For some reason I felt that I would be asked to cover something decent. When I approached the front bulletin board where the assignment sheets are posted, that fire I spoke of quickly extinguished. Stephen Ross heads the Serling High School Newspaper, The Serling Sentinel. He is the senior editor and a year older than me. That has always guaranteed him the choice stories, as well as the benefits that went along with them. He was getting an exclusive with the *Extreme Titans Wrestling Network* that was holding a long-anticipated event at our school this weekend. That included celebrity interviews and all the backstage access.

Shelly Coverdale was the alternate senior editor, also a year older than me. She was tasked with reporting on the sudden rash of stolen cars parked within the vicinity of school property.

Yes People, yours truly, Dennis Sommers was assigned to cover the campaign speech of Benjamin Caxton. Good ol' Ben, a household name, was running for the position of State Senator in our district. The excitement could kill me.

My journey for this story took me to Singleton Baseball Field where patriotism was in full affect, full display, and flapping in a full breeze. A small stage was positioned across one of the playing diamonds with a red white and blue fringe dangling off the edge of it. The breeze was brushing said fringe against the tired green grass below. Miniature American flags were affixed to the stage front, meticulously spaced approximately two feet apart. There was a podium in the center of the stage. A poster adorned the facing of the podium that read *Elect Benjamin Caxton*. The colorful lettering was in red, white, and blue. On top of the podium was a microphone held in place by a serpentine metal coil. Looking to the left and right I noticed public address speakers facing the audience. For the record, they were not colored red, white, or blue, just black.

A sizeable crowd had assembled. Men and women, mostly adults were mingling on the grassy area in front of the stage. A few of them were clutching the hands of small children or had a stroller parked in front of them. A number of them held homemade signs that read *Bean Counter Ben*. Huh? I don't think Ben Caxton worked at the Bean Counter Coffee Shop in town. Perhaps I was missing something. Anyway, a mixture of discussion about the upcoming election filled the air. Many of the conversations began with, "Did you know," or "I heard," or "So and so told me." This was just where I wanted to be today.

As if Mr. Caxton had not drilled his good name into my head already, a giant banner bearing it covered the outfield fence. I stared at it with mixed feelings. Playing the mind association game, I was stuck on the fact that I had participated in two years of Little League and had never hit a baseball near that fence. Recognizing better talents in writing and computers, we can just fast forward to today. Anyhow, my point is Benjamin Caxton had enough campaign promotion to choke a horse.

Getting back to the situation at hand, not only did I have to report on the campaign speech, I was asked to take pictures as well. I am an aspiring journalist, *not* a photographer. As far as I know they never asked any of the other reporters to take pictures, so why me? I think the junior reporter is expected to do many unprecedented things.

Since my last assignment, I had become better equipped. I had upgraded a number of computers for some customers during the week and had made a decent commission. With that commission, I purchased a portable digital voice recorder. With its 512 Megabyte built-in flash memory, I intended to use it today to capture Caxton's speech and dissect it later for my story.

Having used a few digital cameras before I cannot decide which one I prefer, but the school's camera wasn't bad. I removed it from the case and checked out the zoom while keeping my eye on the viewfinder. A group of small children, oblivious to their parents, collectively stuck their tongues at me. That was pleasing. I decided to view find somewhere else. I zoomed on the stage when a voice behind me called out, "No paparazzi allowed!"

I turned suddenly and my eyes lit up at the sight of a face I knew well. Sandra Small. Her auburn hair was illuminating in the afternoon sun. Meanwhile, her green eyes beamed behind the wire-rimmed spectacles that graced a smooth complexion.

"What brings you here," I asked snapping a picture of her.

Cocking an eyebrow at me she replied, "Let's just say I'm taking an interest in the future of our town. I want to hear what this Caxton guy has to say."

I didn't really acknowledge what she said because she was positively glowing in a beige sweater and bright blue jeans. Her eyes seemed to be examining me.

"This is new for you," she said pointing at the camera in my hand and the recorder hanging from a strap around my neck.

I tried to strike a serious pose.

"All in the name of journalism, you know…the quest for the truth."

She shot a vacant stare at me for a moment, then burst out laughing. Composing herself, she affectionately brushed her hand across my hair. The hair only had a modest amount of gel in it today. The laws of gravity were in firm place because it was doing anything but spiking upward, a look I was desperately trying to achieve. Not cool.

In an attempt to draw attention off my unruly hair, I quickly changed the conversation. I got back to the subject at hand.

"Hey, you work at the Bean Counter. Does Ben Caxton own it or something? I see all these signs around here."

She started to crack up.

My confused look prompted her to say, "He's fiscally sound. He knows how to watch the dollar and save money."

"Got it," I replied grinding my teeth.

"I'm going to get a closer look," she said walking toward the front of the stage. "Check you out later."

The event was about to start and I was glad that my embarrassing question was now behind me.

A lanky man that I pegged for about forty-five years old approached the podium. A creaking noise amplified over the speakers as he bent the threaded mount that was holding the microphone to his level.

"Ladies and gentleman, it is my pleasure to introduce the next Senator of the 11th district, the future of this town. Let's hear it for Benjamin Caxton!"

Applause filled the baseball field as people raised their signs and Caxton shook hands with the announcer. He stepped up to the podium, smiles galore. He looked in good shape for his age, which the biography on his website listed as fifty. He was neat in his appearance. A hint of gray in his hair was hardly noticeable and gave him a wiser looking image.

I engaged the voice recorder to capture Mr. Caxton as he said, "Good afternoon." His arms spread outward as the crowd collectively returned his greeting. His introduction went on for a few minutes and then he segued into a new topic. "I now want to focus on the importance of protecting our environmental resources and how in doing so, we can ensure a better today and a brighter tomorrow." This drew some more applause as his arms again spread outward.

Tilting the recorder upward, I looked at the facing to see the time counter passing nine minutes. Funny, it seemed to me like I was standing here for an hour. When he broke into commentary on health care for senior citizens, I began to look for something to hold my interest.

He started to talk about his opponent. I'm certain the current Senator, Senator Hildebrand, wasn't something you'd find in a *salad*, pretty sure he wasn't a *vegetable*. Either way before I wrote my article I would be sure to look up the definition of the word incumbent, because it sounded an awful lot like *cucumber*. Coffee beans, cucumbers, politics is a strange field.

Next was a brief bit on learning resources. Learning usually means work, so I tuned out for a minute. Nevertheless, I perked up when Caxton mentioned channeling additional funds for computers already available at the public library.

I decided to mess around with the digital camera. Discovering the toggle switch that activated the zoom, I started working it. I was zooming in and out and all around, invading people's space without them even knowing it. Very cool! Then that nasty Mrs. Floyd *grossed me out* by picking her nose just as I zoomed in her direction. *Ewww*!! I think she was eating the findings. Quick I thought, zoom somewhere else. The podium seemed like a safe place. Caxton was talking about renovating the town parks. Again, his arms extended outward...and remained outward. I zoomed in closer. He was in mid-sentence when I wondered if I was the only one who noticed a patch of red dripping from behind his left ear.

The collective scream of the people was haunting as Benjamin

Caxton toppled off the stage taking the whole podium with him. As if a giant bus was grinding its brakes, a screeching noise filled the air. Caxton's body was sprawled across the microphone, causing a horrendous feedback that was rattling the speakers. I was familiar with that sound having seen my friend Theo Russell's hard rock band play a few times. It was a lot to take in at once, but the realization finally hit me,

Benjamin Caxton was shot!

I was about forty feet away from him, standing on legs that I swear were not mine. Doing the only thing I could think to do, I took pictures. I snapped away. Morbid? Not really. I couldn't get close enough to help and a number of people were on cell phones presumably calling 911. Parents with young children were rushing back toward the street. Other folks seemed frozen with their hands covering gaping mouths.

It was my story and it ended up being the scene of a shooting. One problem, I saw no shooter! Looking in the field area behind the stage, I saw nothing. Looking through the viewfinder I used the zoom to see further away. Still no one! I continued taking pictures anyway.

Looking down, I remembered the recorder around my neck. Sirens were filling the air as I turned it off. Looking back up, I saw several uniformed police officers storming the field in the company of a few Emergency Medical Technicians.

The lead officer was crouching next to the medic that was examining the body of Benjamin Caxton, while others were a flurry of motion on the field. Some were securing a perimeter around the body while others were questioning witnesses for any immediate information.

A stretcher appeared from somewhere and Caxton's shuddering body was being placed upon it. I noticed the man who introduced him next to the medics trying to hold Caxton in place. A police officer was hollering something into a radio clutched in his left hand.

An ambulance was pulling onto the field. I found myself staring as the body shook violently.

The cops on the scene remained poised, heads turning from side-to-side as if they were expecting something. Oh..., I know what they were expecting. Walking onto the field was a headstrong twosome I had the displeasure of meeting recently. Detectives Withers and Riley. Again, they were wearing identical suits. I'm telling you they must buy them at a two-for-one store and split the cost of the one.

I looked around and it did not seem like many people had left. The crowd looked bigger with the added police presence. I couldn't find Sandra as I saw yellow crime scene tape being taken out by one of the boys in blue.

I decided to leave, but emergency personnel gummed up the entrance to the ball field. I wanted out of this place with a little less resistance. I walked in the opposite direction staying far to the right of the stage. I kept going around the outfield fence where the baseball grounds gave way to an undeveloped, heavily wooded area. I knew it eventually let out onto one of the neighborhood cross streets.

I was walking on eggshells, totally expecting to hear someone shout out, "Stop that guy!" Luckily, that did not happen.

The confusion was clouding my judgment. As I got closer to the trees and high grass, I wondered if I should have stayed. Avoiding wild shrubbery and displaced nature, I realized there was nothing I could do. I was also well aware that the Serling High editorial head assigned me the Benjamin Caxton speech prior to these developments. It was my story!

Maybe if I had hung around I might have heard some important information. Then again, the police might start detaining witnesses and I only saw what everyone else saw. I needed to regroup, to get my facts straight, and to pick someone's brain. First, I decided the regrouping would be done on Baskerville Street. Second, the brain belonged to Matthew Livingston. The third thing was getting my facts. I was clueless. I picked up my pace.

CHAPTER 2

I ALWAYS FOUND IT a bit spooky. I was referring to the detached garage next to the home of Matthew Livingston. I entered it via the side door and made my way up the staircase to the loft.

As my sneakers reached the top step, I could see my friend tending to some of the much-used glassware in his makeshift laboratory. He was the only seventeen year old I knew who had an avid interest in chemistry, a subject most of us in school dreaded. Not him; he spent hours upon hours studying it. Recently he had used some of that knowledge of chemistry to expose a black market weapons' builder and solve an almost overlooked homicide of a philanthropist. It was an account I jotted down in my journal and cleverly, by my own standards, titled *The Millionaire Murder*.

My sneakers squeaked on the wood floor of the loft. Matthew must have heard them because he looked up suddenly in my direction. He was wearing his white overcoat. His hands, covered in brown work gloves, clutched a glass beaker high in the air as his narrow eyes coolly stared over it. The eyes were framed by slightly long dark hair that dangled from the sides of his head. The intensity of his look was accompanied by a pronounced exhale.

"What did you do *now*?"

I stepped lightly toward the large wooden wheel top that sat in the middle of the loft. On one side of this rough and ready table was a tattered yellow sofa. On the other side was a pair of metal folding chairs. Recently, Matthew, Sandra, and I had logged in quite a bit of time in this place, using it as a staging area during our last escapade. I sat in one of the chairs with the wheel top behind me, facing him as he arranged items on an old metal shelving unit in the rear of the loft.

I started my story from the beginning when I received my journalism assignment at school. He started positioning different sized glasses on one of the shelves. As I explained the set up down at Singleton Baseball Field, he continued messing with the glasses. I gave him the background about being asked to take pictures and doing so. When I got to the part where Caxton took the stage, he interrupted me.

"Do you know what the word *vex* means?"

His question caught me off guard. My shoulders raised slightly on their own, supporting the blank look on my face.

"No, I don't know what the word vex….."

My eyes squinted somewhat and then got large. That was when I made out the thick, flat black object that was sailing towards my head. It was the last second, but I managed to duck in time. Behind me, a loud *thud* rang out. I turned around and in the middle of the wheel top was a dictionary. Okay, I understood what this meant so I grasped it in my hands and flipped and flipped. His back was to me when I found the section for the letter V. He made a spinning motion with his right hand that I interpreted as his request for me to either hurry up or read aloud.

"Vex," I said in a clear voice, "to irritate, to annoy, to…."

"Exactly what you do every time you come *here*!"

Wow, I thought still holding the dictionary. He certainly was a loner. He really didn't desire the company of others. Still I needed to finish my story in a way I hoped would capture his attention.

"Benjamin Caxton wasn't ten minutes into his speech when he was shot!"

His eyebrows rose.

"Did you say *shot*?"

This was a first. I actually did get his attention. I quickly reported what I saw, from the blood dripping, to Caxton collapsing, when Livingston turned quickly toward the shelving unit he had been arranging.

Reaching up on top of it, he pulled a white cloth off of something. An old transistor radio was revealed. He grabbed it.

"I didn't actually hear a shot ring out or anything but…"

"*Silencers*," his whisper added a sudden chill that hung like a veil over the room.

I could not believe the suddenness of his interest or enthusiasm.

How quickly his mood could transition. Hurriedly spinning knobs on the old radio, a crackle of static filled the loft and morphed into the voice of a news announcer.

"Again, if you are just joining us, Benjamin Caxton, candidate for Senate in the eleventh district, was shot by what appears to be a sniper, while giving a campaign speech at the Singleton Little League Field. He remains in critical condition at Lakeville County Hospital. The police currently have no one in custody. In other news…"

A sharp *click* ended the transmission as Matthew turned the radio off and placed it back on the shelf. He turned slowly toward me and shut his eyes so tight his cheeks wrinkled. He was wearing a button down white shirt under the lab coat. As usual, his tan slacks were perfectly creased, right down to the brown suede shoes he wore.

"You said you were taking pictures."

My right hand found its way into the inner pocket of my trusty blue denim jacket. The digital camera was there.

"Yeah," I replied, "I did take some pictures. And I did an audio recording with this," I said holding up the digital voice recorder.

"Can we preview the pictures?"

"Sure," I said slipping the camera out of its case.

As I removed it, I felt a vibration in my right front pants pocket.

It was my cell phone. Someone was texting me. I read the message and shoved the phone back into my pocket.

"That was Sandra; she's parked down the block. Apparently, our favorite detectives are on their way up here now. I forgot to mention. Withers and Riley responded to the shooting today."

He moved quickly towards me and said, "Pull the memory card out of the camera and give it to me."

His sense of urgency propelled me to rapidly remove the small square chip from a side panel of the camera. Tossing it to Matthew, he jammed it into his left front pants pocket, without saying a word.

Not a second later, I heard the squeaking of the wooden stairs in the loft. We had company.

Matthew gazed sharply at the two intruders. They had paid us a visit here once before and the surroundings had the same effect on them. They looked around with puzzled expressions before their eyes settled on us.

It was Riley, with his head still looking like it was carved out of butter, who spoke first.

"You," he demanded. "What were you doing at that baseball field today?"

Matthew was actually smiling as he answered for me, "Didn't you two learn from our last encounter? He's sixteen years old. You can't interrogate him without a parent or guardian present."

"Common right of inquiry," Withers barked back.

"That tone in his voice," Matthew said, pointing at Riley, "sounded like an interrogation to me."

"Common right of inquiry," he repeated himself.

"Not a chance. And for your information, the bus doesn't stop here, so *go now!*"

Withers marched his barrel chest closer to Matt and said, "We'll *go* when we get some information."

"If I'm not mistaken you two specialize in homicides, am I correct? Your day begins when someone else's ends. I am in the ballpark here, right? So I take it by your presence Benjamin Caxton has gone out of the picture."

"The only pictures we want to know about are the ones he was taking," Riley punctuated his response by pointing at me.

I fought the urge not to smile. I realized Matthew had the memory card for the camera in his pocket and these two would be up a tree shortly.

Withers very arrogantly asked, "Any special reason why you're always around when people get killed, like that *millionaire* a few weeks ago."

I sighed and stupidly explained myself, "My school newspaper asked me to cover the campaign speech. I'm fairly certain they didn't tell me to cover the campaign speech because someone would be shot."

"Fork over the camera," Riley demanded.

I had already placed the camera securely in its black case. I flipped it to Riley.

"This is evidence," he said clumsily catching it with two hands.

"Then," Matthew said overly pronounced in a tone I can now describe as vexing, "I assume you'll be giving Dennis Sommers a receipt?"

"He can get it down at the precinct," he retorted.

The two of them in their twin suits turned and made their way out of the loft.

I could hear the door on the side of the garage closing. Matt's eyelids lowered. He appeared to be listening. Perhaps he was making sure our guests had left. His head snapped toward me as he broke his silence.

"You said Sandra is close by, yes?"

I settled on the yellow sofa trying to guess where he was going with his question.

"She is."

"Take that phone out of your pocket and call her. We need her here."

I stood up, fully understanding the determination in his voice. I took it out and called Sandra.

"What's going on," she asked, with a voice that suggested she was in concern mode.

"Our friends are gone. Can you get over here, to the loft?"

"I'm down the block. What's up?"

"The Genius wants you."

"I'm there!"

Two minutes later the lovely and talented Sandra Small entered the coaxingly creative workspace of Matthew Livingston. The loft once again appeared to be emerging as ground zero for another predicament. Hopefully, solace and solutions would again surface.

"What gives," she asked while looking at the two of us.

"I appreciate the tip-off," Matthew said. "Those two clowns saw Dennis taking pictures at the shooting and came here to confiscate his camera."

"So they did," as her eyes got tiny behind the wire-rimmed specs.

"Thanks to you I took the liberty of removing this," Matthew indicated as he displayed the memory card, holding it high between two fingers.

She smiled.

"What now," I asked, sensing the weight of another criminal case shifting onto my shoulders.

"Sandra," he addressed her, "can you take Dennis to the precinct to get a receipt for the camera?"

"Of course."

"We can just let it go," I suggested imploringly. "I'll tell the school tomorrow and let them deal with it."

"No, I need you down there appearing concerned about the camera," Matthew responded firmly. "They are bound to discover the memory card missing when they examine it. I need you to insist it was in there when you gave it to them and it must be a convincing performance."

"This might be fun," Sandra said with an edge of delight, "I'm in."

I wasn't sure what I was getting into, but again I was clearly outnumbered. And, now *I* felt vexed.

"You must *go now*," he spoke boldly, "check in with me later."

Raising myself from the tattered couch, I reluctantly followed Sandra from the loft to her car.

CHAPTER 3

THE POLICE STATION HAS not changed since my last visit. It is still a two-story structure of sorts, in dire need of a paint job. The strong smell of disinfectant jogged my memory back a few weeks ago when I spent some time here unwillingly. The circumstances were a little less stressful this time. Nevertheless, I had to take into consideration that Riley and Withers might start harassing me once they discovered the memory card was missing.

Withers was the one that I had to deal with first. He was seated at a small metal table. He could barely fit his legs underneath it. On top of the table was an old electric typewriter. He was sliding a carbon copy form into the typewriter. I glanced over and scanned the top of the form. *Property Clerk Invoice.* There was a serialized number on top of the form prefixed with the letter R. I really didn't understand the form, but I needed a receipt and apparently this was the receipt.

I looked over at Sandra who was staring at something. Quickly, I took notice. Two detectives were directing a young man, wearing a leather vest over a denim jacket, into the holding cell. He was a member of a motorcycle gang called the *Savage Swords and Skulls.* We saw them in action not too long ago.

"Last name," Withers asked me with zero emotion.

"You must be joking," I laughed. I knew he was well acquainted with my last name after my previous interaction with him. Realizing

I might be in for a long afternoon, I told him my last name and spelled it out for him. He typed. His hands crashed down on the keys one at a time.

"First name?"

I gave him that too. Again, *crash, crash.*

"Address?"

I could not believe it. He had no problem finding my house a few weeks ago. I gave him the address on Brenner Lane as he went on typing methodically. The machine was clacking at a tedious pace. Honestly, this guy must have typed hundreds of these things. You would think he would be faster with his fingertips.

No such luck.

Sandra was behind me nudging my right shoulder. I turned to look and observed Detective Riley, examining the digital camera. He was holding it at an arms' distance as if it were contaminated.

I realized I was staring a bit long. Not wanting to arouse suspicion, I turned back to Withers.

"Hey Bruce," he called over. "Let me see that thing."

I thought that he would at least be searching for images to view, but no. He began typing the description of the camera on a line that read *Item 1, Quantity 1.* This included such things as the serial number. His teeth were grinding, while his eyes were glued to the keys of the typewriter. *Crash.* Again, his fingers pounded down. It was actually somewhat amusing to watch this oversized officer of the law, sandwiched under a desk pounding away at paperwork.

Withers finished typing. Pulling the form out, he walked it over to a desk in the rear of the office where an older man, in a wrinkled brown suit was affixed. He looked like an appendage of the place in his outdated suit and tired expression. I recognized him from my last visit. He looked over the form, signed it, and handed it back to Withers, who gave me my copy.

I faced the door meaning to leave, but Sandra headed in the opposite direction. She stopped next to Withers who seemed to be having an outer body experience staring at the typewriter.

"They train animals to type faster than that!"

She shot the remark at him so fast it was wasted on him. He was staring at the typewriter as if he were being asked to perform open-heart surgery. Scary.

Leaving the squad room, we walked down an old concrete staircase. When we reached the bottom there was quite a commotion. Pushing open the heavy door in front of me my eyes were set back. The entire entrance to the precinct was crowded with people.

The press!

A number of men were carrying video equipment and others were holding lighting gear. I recognized two women in front of the stationhouse desk. They were news reporters; I just could not remember what networks they represented. Both of them were gripping microphones.

I looked over at the Desk Sergeant who was standing behind his mantle furiously calling for order, his attempts clearly faltering. Sandra and I inched closer, completely unnoticed, into the fracas.

We were standing to the side of a geeky looking dude with square framed glasses who was holding his head up as if he had not slept in days. In a bellyaching voice he complained, "What time are they going to do this?"

Sandra mockingly asked him, "Can I get you some cheese to go with that whine?"

He looked like he was close to tears. We slipped past the entourage and out the front door.

Stopping in front of her car Sandra asked, "What do we need to do?"

"Swing by my place. I'll grab my laptops, a card reader, and some accessories."

"It looks like a press conference is going to eventually take place."

"Yeah, I can get all the news channels. They stream live online, so we can watch. I brought my backup laptop home from school so we can run two at a time."

"Good idea. Kid Genius should be interested in this. At least we can see how far the cops have gotten."

Sandra started up the car and headed in the direction of Brenner Lane, the home of yours truly.

Having secured the necessary items, Sandra drove back to the loft. The mood was still the same over there, strange.

I placed both laptops on the center wheel top and fired them up. Placing a duffel bag filled with accessories on the floor, I dropped onto the yellow sofa and positioned the computers in front of me. Doing a quick search for our regular news networks, I found their corresponding web sites. It read '*Standing by for Police press conference on the shooting of Benjamin Caxton*'.

I clicked the link and it indicated the feed would go live when the conference started. Turning my attention to the other laptop, I did the same search on another local news station and they had a similar message.

Matthew emerged from the rear of the loft. He wore neither a lab coat, nor gloves or safety glasses. He settled in on my right, with Sandra on my left, one leg tucked under her.

Waiting on the press conference, I decided to plug in the card reader to one of the computers. Icons appeared on the screen and I clicked on the first one to enlarge it. There was my first picture of Sandra. She looked great with the sunshine bouncing off her hair. I advanced to the next shot. Like opening the floodgates of drama, I was revisited by the events at Singleton Field that afternoon.

The first couple of pictures were as expected. Images of the stage and the people stretched across the laptop screen. I wasn't exactly sure what would come next. I remembered soon enough as the carnage of the afternoon revealed itself in contrast and color saturation. The result was bold and brilliant images of Benjamin Caxton collapsing.

I turned away as Matthew got closer to the screen. He was completely unphased. He seemed to have no problem separating himself from the graphic nature of what was being displayed.

"How can you look at that?"

"Objectively," he replied still staring in. "I want copies of these. All of them."

"I can burn you a disc?"

His head shook slightly, side-to-side.

"No. I want prints. Prints I can hold in my hands and examine. I may not always have the luxury of a computer to view them on."

I grabbed the duffel bag off the floor and removed a compact photo printer. I opened a fresh pack of photo cards and loaded them into the base of the printer. Connecting the USB cable, within minutes, I began running off copies.

"Aren't you glad you have me around," I joked while the printer kicked out pictures.

"No," he said flatly.

After his reply, which did anything but surprise me, I noticed the press conference was starting. A reporter's voice, with contained excitement, stated, "We now take you live to the press conference."

The scene was somewhere inside the precinct and in the center of the room was a podium. I was somewhat certain no one standing behind this podium would get shot. Behind it, I recognized the older man from the squad room. He was the supervisor of our favorite detectives. Clearing his throat a bit too long for my listening pleasure, he began to speak. The brown wrinkled suit portrayed him for television viewing as quite the mess.

His mouth was moving and I could not hear a thing he was saying. I increased the laptops volume control and still nothing above a mumble.

"Do you think he can speak up," Sandra asked with some frustration.

"He has nothing to say," Matthew answered her, fixated on the screen. "He's completely confused."

"How do you know that?"

He just made four indications with his body. I've studied

behavioral reactions and let's just say he's a text book example of confusion."

Finally, he found his voice.

"For more on this matter I give you Detective Bruce Riley."

My good buddy approached the podium as news reporters thrust microphones in his direction. His smug face gave way to an equally smug voice.

"Ben Caxton, candidate for Senator in the 11ᵗʰ District, was pronounced dead at 3:45 p.m. today at Lakeville County Hospital. We are currently interviewing witnesses and rest assured we are compiling detailed information about today's shooting. We are confident we will have the shooter in custody before long."

A cacophony of voices became very audible and Riley pointed toward the group.

A woman's voice asked, "What information have you gathered?"

"We have explored numerous possibilities in our investigation so far."

Matthew commented with much sarcasm, "Caxton died at 3:45 p.m. today and this man has numerous possibilities explored. I will explore a possibility. It's just possible that he's lying!"

Riley continued, "While we can't divulge all of our investigative details, we can inform you that only one bullet was fired. It entered the back of Benjamin Caxton's head just above his left ear. Ballistics has the round and we believe there is revealing evidence connected to it."

"I'm sure the shooter carved his initials in the base of the bullet," Matthew said dryly to the image of Detective Riley on the computer screen.

"We are examining military records as the shooting resembles the marksmanship of a trained shooter. We are confident in our Department's diligent pursuit and again, we hope to have this person in custody very soon."

The screen flashed to a man at the television studio. "We will break away from the press conference at this time and return when we have an update."

The other news station didn't break away and the three of us turned our attention to it, raising the volume. There were a few mumbled questions that Riley was answering with a 'yes' or a 'no' before that station broke away as well.

Sandra and I turned to look at our friend. His head was reclined and he was staring up into the ceiling of the loft.

"What do you think of Riley's comments?"

"Idiot," he whispered.

"Why do you say that?"

"Because he is!"

The printing had completed and Matthew took the stack of photos and walked to the rear of the loft. He stopped in front of the old metal shelving and his right hand grasped a roll of masking tape from it. He was taping the pictures to the frame of the shelving. All of them. He even taped up the picture I had taken of Sandra. I was quite sure he didn't share the same attraction to her that I did, or did he?

He stared at the pictures as if he was trying to see through them. I studied him for a moment, motionless he seemed to me. Finally, I detected movement as muscles formed lines around the corner of his mouth. I didn't know if he was grinding his teeth or what, but suddenly something was forced out.

"Hack!"

"What," Sandra and I asked simultaneously.

"I said hack, a word in *your* vocabulary I presume?"

"Yes," I stood up and gazed at him, trying to guess where he was going with this. "I'm capable in the area of hacking." It dawned on me that there wasn't much else I felt capable in, except my writing.

"Hold that thought," he said turning to face us, "until tomorrow or Wednesday perhaps." A faint light bulb overhead was illuminating the solemn look on his face. I wish a light bulb would appear over my head, which would indicate that I had a clue as to what he was thinking about now.

It was he and I standing. Sandra still sat. We looked around at each other. The silence surrounding us in the loft was chasing a chill up my spine. I knew it was dark out and that was adding a dour feeling to this dilemma. Danger was at our door. Again.

He broke the silence.

"We've seen first hand how our favorite detectives have entertained a false conclusion. This time if that happens I fear greater consequences."

Sandra asked, "What are you thinking?"

"I have a theory. We will discuss it tomorrow."

"You want to meet before school, back door?"

"Yes. Bring a few newspapers as you've done before. Must see what the press knows. You also said you made an audio recording of the speech. I need a copy of that."

I started to power down my laptops and collect my accessories. I looked at him, hesitated, and then asked, "Anything else?"

"One thing," he said in a sharp, serious tone. His hand motioned to the shelf behind him that was now decorated with the pictures I took. "As long as these are in my possession I must keep the garage locked. If our friends drop in and discover them..." he did not finish the sentence. "If you need me, there is a bell outside. Use it!"

Sandra picked up one of the laptops and I the other. We headed towards the stairs. I paused shortly to look at Matthew Livingston. In the poorly lit loft, he stood tall with his hands behind his back. He was staring at the pictures.

CHAPTER 4

GAZING IN THE MIRROR the next morning, I assured myself that it was indeed me. I forced a comb through my bangs in an upward motion. I had applied a strong gel. Dropping the comb in the sink, I quickly turned on the hair dryer I had ready at my side. I fired away with hot air, and then, fired away some more. Turning the dryer off, I looked in the mirror as the hair and all my hopes collapsed.

Perhaps I'm just slow on the uptake of things or still recovering from the shock of seeing a man murdered. After I had packed up all my computer gear last night, I went home and fell asleep quickly, exhausted from the day's events. About a minute into the examination of my inner eyelids, I snapped them open to a realization. We were withholding evidence in a murder investigation. Matthew Livingston really freaked me out this time. I had seen him push the envelope with the police previously. Was he treating this as a personal contest or something? Honestly, with all the resources the police have, could he find the shooter any faster than them? I was not about to ask him. I would have another book thrown at me for sure. I just wanted to know what he was getting at. I was certain this wasn't a race to justice. He would not engage in a battle of wits for the glory of it. Or, would he? Since meeting him, he was quite the opposite inasmuch as he didn't own up to his work.

Leaving the house, I switched out of this thought pattern when I saw the crimson red Ford Mustang turn onto Brenner Lane, stopping in front of my house. Climbing in the passenger's seat, I greeted Sandra. She wore a black knit cap on her head and an almost gold colored sweater was visible under a dark blue denim jacket. She was going through the gears of the muscular vehicle and in a few minutes, we hit a main avenue. Finding the closest convenience store, she pulled into the parking lot. Hopping out, I made for the store.

Inside, I grabbed two city edition papers and the county paper as well. Dropping a buck and a half on the counter that was muddled with candy and other junk I rejoined Sandra and we made our way to school.

As she drove, I perused the newspapers. The first one had a headline that read, **"CANDIDATE SHOT BY SNIPER"**. The color photo under it showed crime scene tape with police and paramedics surrounding the area of Singleton Baseball Field. The second paper I glanced at had the same photograph but the headline read *coldly*, **"CROSSED OFF THE BALLOT"**. A photo of a smiling Caxton accompanied it. The third paper's headline pertained to a completely different story, but there was a small article about the Caxton shooting on page three.

There wasn't much interaction at the back door of Serling High. I handed off the newspapers to Matt. He glanced at the headlines and told us to meet him at the auditorium before fifth period.

Once in school, I walked to the first floor classroom where Mr. C setup shop for the school newspaper. When I arrived, I felt cheated. Scrawled across the chalkboard was a message saying Mr.C would be out for the day. I mean honestly, I was expecting maybe a week off for trauma. Me, Dennis Sommers, assigned a story for the paper sees a man shot dead. Anyhow, it was useless. All I was going to do was explain to him what happened and ask if he wanted me to go on with the story. I wanted to go on with the story, but given the unexpected turn of events, it seemed likely the story might be dropped.

After fourth period ended, I made quick time to the auditorium. As I approached the side door, I thought maybe our little meeting was not to be. I heard a piano playing and remembered that the school's chorus class sometimes used the auditorium for rehearsing. Peering inside, I was surprised to see Sandra seated at the baby grand.

Now this was a bizarre scene. She was sitting, back straight, playing a classical piece. Sitting in the front row, immersed in concentration, was Matthew Livingston. His eyes closed, his hands together, he seemed in an almost prayer like position. She stopped playing and looked up at me.

"Fast cars, motorcycle jumping, classical piano…"

"I'll have you know I'm a relative of the great Michael Garson."

"Any other hidden talents?"

She stood up from the bench in an exaggerated poise. Turning slightly, her back bent forward and both hands went flat to the floor. In an instant, her feet were straight in the air. Then as gracefully as they went up, they returned to the shiny auditorium floor.

"It's easier with ballet slippers, but you won't catch me dead wearing them."

I began to applaud.

"*Urrrghh…*"

The noise came from Livingston whose eyes were still closed.

His voice was calm as he spoke, "I've reviewed the papers. The police have a theory on the shooter being someone who was in the military. Someone possibly discharged dishonorably and who might have a grudge against elected officials, who have been openly supportive of war initiatives. They are currently checking records beginning with the residents of our district."

"Sounds like a good lead," I replied unsure of just what I was saying.

"What it sounds like," he said pausing slightly, "is a convenient solution."

"True," Sandra agreed, "you could even get some whacko to confess to that for the publicity alone."

I thought about what she said, yet could not imagine someone actually doing that. Confessing to a murder they didn't commit for some attention?

"The police have chosen to pigeon-hole their investigation; we will not do the same."

"Why are you so interested in this," I interjected.

He didn't move. He didn't even look up at me. He replied solemnly, "I believe it was not that long ago in this very same room I told you something about murder and consequence."

My breathing stopped slightly as I wished I hadn't asked that question. Realizing he did not jump down my throat, it started to dawn on me that he might actually be tired. Perhaps he was up all night studying those pictures I took.

"I remember what you said."

It was true. I had thought about it often since that day. When one human being murders another, there are ramifications that affect *many* others. There certainly was a domino effect in the case of Malcolm Everest, a former journalism subject of mine, who met an untimely fate. Perhaps whatever length someone went to in order to murder Benjamin Caxton, candidate for Senator, greater intentions lay in wait.

"Instructions," Sandra asked.

He was motionless, but his voice moved with an unnerving authority.

"Check in with me this evening. Remember unless something changes, the door to the garage will be locked. Use the bell!"

He walked out of the auditorium, but the mysterious aura surrounding the room remained. I looked at Sandra and she joined me as we headed to class.

CHAPTER 5

AFTER SCHOOL, I TOOK care of some things at home and packed a bag with some equipment for that evening. Among the usual computer accessories, I included a copy of the CD that I burned from the mini-disc recorder; I also saved a copy on my desktop. Having some time before visiting Matthew in the evening, I decided to drop by Sandra at her job. Perhaps she could clear my clouds of confusion on this matter.

The *Bean Counter* was a pleasurable coffee shop Sandra worked at and Benjamin Caxton did not own. I visited often and wrote my articles for the school paper or performed other writing tasks here. It was a creative environment. Now give me some credit because I usually brought a notebook to scribble some rough drafts. I never actually set up a laptop and typed away. I never understood the people that did that. I would stop in for coffee and there would be some person who would take over a table with his laptop. He would grunt and groan away as he typed, begging to be noticed. Then he would usually utter some comment like, "This screenplay is going to be the death of me." My philosophy was the writing came first and the written word was best channeled from pen to paper. That was what people would ultimately see, the printed word. You write to be *read*, not to be seen.

Anyhow, as I entered there was only one person today at a table in the middle. He had a frothy mug of something next to his laptop. I looked past him and spotted Sandra who was fixing a component on a cappuccino machine. Her sleeves were rolled up as her pale hands grasped a shiny metal spout of some sort. She was crouched low looking up into the apparatus.

"Okay," she said still staring in, "the steam valve is clear now. Give it a whirl."

The young man behind the counter placed a small cup in the well of the machine and hit a button on the side of it. Sandra stood behind him, rolling down her sleeves as espresso dispensed normally.

"Thanks," he said to her as she lifted two orange ceramic mugs.

"I'd run off five or six cups, it's been sitting for a bit."

Her co-worker frowned replying, "At four bucks for an espresso the owner's gonna love that."

"He can deduct it from my service bill; I'm taking fifteen minutes with my friend," she said jerking her thumb in my direction.

I sat at one of the café tables and Sandra appeared opposite me, placing two mugs on the table that bore the shop's logo. She had a dispenser of brown organic sugar and added some to her coffee.

"Well," I began after thanking her, "you'll be relieved to know that no one was shot on my way over here." I was desperately trying to make light of the last twenty-four hours.

She laughed and we clanked the mugs together. I glanced around at the customers who seemed self-absorbed, texting on cell phones while listening to MP3 players. The smell of French vanilla and baked goods wrestled for control of my senses.

"Certainly not me," she responded, "I drive too fast."

She was unique. She was self-reliant, yet humorous. I must have appeared a little edgy in her presence and understandably so. She noticed.

"What's wrong?"

I realized I was tapping the side of the mug with my forefinger, so I stopped.

"Caxton's shooting compounded with Livingston's antics. It's enough to torment my nervous system."

"Hey," she said, lowering her voice, "I saw the guy get shot too. It's crazy. You never think something like this would happen in your own town and right before your own eyes."

"True. Combine that with the tension of having the police harassing me over my journalism assignment...again. It makes for a miserable time."

"Have they noticed the memory card for the camera missing yet?"

"I guess not," I said wearily. "That's another thing I'm not ready for either.

"You need to be, it's bound to happen and soon."

"Fortunately they have no idea about the mini disc recording or I'm sure they would have demanded that as well. I need to pay the Genius a visit. I'm confused."

"Okay," she said sipping from the mug. "I finish here at seven. I'll meet you over at the loft after that."

"That sounds good. I'm in the dark here. Any idea why he is so determined on this one?"

"Like before, he appears to have discovered something and he's not ready just yet to inform us. Hang in there. Maybe tonight we'll have a clearer picture."

I finished my coffee and thanked her again.

CHAPTER 6

IT WAS DARK AS I approached the detached garage next to the Livingston home. I went to reach for the door and remembered that Matthew was keeping it locked. Feeling around next to the doorframe, I found the bell. Pressing my thumb against it, I waited. In a minute, I could see the top of his head peering out a small window on the garage door. He opened it quickly. Once inside, I watched him close and lock it twice as quick.

Upstairs in the loft, it was much the same as when I left it yesterday, with the exception of a stepladder in the center. Matthew climbed up and quickly changed the bulb. The room became brighter. My eyes adjusted and I looked down at the wheel top and noticed a late edition newspaper.

A buzzing sound rang out. It was the bell as Matt descended the stairs. The lovely and multi-talented Sandra Small entered the loft with Matthew behind her. She was carrying a box with coffee cups and two bags in it.

"Anything from the police yet," she asked.

"No," I replied, "I haven't heard from them."

Matthew walked around Sandra to the yellow sofa and sat down. "I believe they have something else they're occupied with."

He flipped open the newspaper and turned it in our direction.

His eyes were sullen as he looked up at us and declared, "The game has begun."

I leaned in a bit closer and so did Sandra. The article was titled "Caxton Killer Speaks!" There was a page worth of paragraphs with a picture of Benjamin Caxton. There was also a reproduction of a handwritten letter. It read,

To our fine Police force and
wonderful people of this community I
speak. It gives pleasure to re-
move some true cancer from our society.
Don't thank me, just understand me.
I walk alone most days; I conceal myself in
time. So do not look for me, you couldn't
find me if you tried. Do not envy me, just
thank me.

It was unsigned and it was freaky!

Sandra grabbed one of the folding chairs and reversed it. Leaning forward, her arms dangled over the chair backing. Underneath the black knit cap, green eyes narrowed in the direction of Matthew Livingston.

"So what happens now," She asked picking up one of the coffee containers. "Does this person wake up on the wrong side of the bed and start picking off community leaders?"

Sitting down as well, I needed some logic, "Let me get this straight. He or she shoots Benjamin Caxton, disappears into thin air, and now wants to start waxing philosophy in a letter sent to the police and the public."

"You can stop expounding on the shooter's gender Dennis. It is a *man*."

I barked, "How do you know?"

"You read the same newspaper I read. Two items give it away, not to mention the handwriting displayed is identifiable to me as a male's penmanship. That is if the shooter wrote the letter himself, but who would he ask to compose something so culpable?"

I wondered if I should ask and decided to jump right in. "The handwriting, something else you studied?"

"Yes. I find it the most revealing insight into a person."

Sandra said, "I think he's pretty stupid for writing the letter. Why do that?"

Matthew gazed at her and replied, "He's not that stupid."

"How so," I asked.

Matt spun the paper around to face him and said, "The line here reads I walk alone most days; I conceal myself in time. He knew enough to separate the two thoughts, independent clauses, with a semicolon. That is a commonly misused form of punctuation. So I say not stupid, but perhaps an exhibitionist?"

"He wants attention," Sandra asked still narrow-eyed.

"Oh, he's got it."

I was in the process of firing up my laptop when Matthew walked to the rear of the loft. A moment later, he appeared holding a magnifying glass. He sat on the sofa and bent over the newspaper. He peered through the glass at the reproduction of the written letter.

"I'm diving into some search engines to see what we know about Benjamin Caxton," I informed him. "Maybe something can shed light on why someone would want to kill him?"

"Okay," Sandra said. "That's a good start. I do feel that we are casting a net into a large sea, but…"

"But its still water," answered Matthew, glued to that magnifying glass.

I got several hits on the computer. Caxton apparently had enjoyed a long career in public service, which was well followed by the media over the years. I started with the news articles.

"Well it says here as of the morning of his death, he was sitting pretty with the popular vote. He was the odds on favorite to win the election."

"Did his opponent shoot him," Sandra asked, deadpanned and straight-faced.

Matthew looked up from the magnifying glass, shot her an odd glance, and returned to the newspaper.

I read on, "Always well-received by the public, never negatively spoke of. The only dirt dished on him was four years ago when he was investigated for income tax fraud. The allegations appear to have been dismissed."

Sandra again, "That does it for me. I think the IRS shot him."

Matthew shook his head slightly.

I went to his own site where he listed a number of proposals. "According to this, he was promising all new roads on main thoroughfares, as well as intersecting and adjacent roads. He promised to expand parks and recreation. One plan would begin immediately to tear down the defunct town water tower and develop the area for a soccer field. Another plan would be to build up existing parks and add new softball fields and indoor/outdoor tennis courts."

I glanced in Sandra's direction for some rebuttal, but this time she had none. She shrugged her shoulders.

Matthew finished looking through the magnifying glass.

"Let's play the recording you made."

I opened the copy saved on my desktop in a program I had that was for audio editing and enhancement.

Turning the laptop to him I explained, "It's showing you the recording in waveform."

"Interesting," he remarked staring at the screen.

Green lines expanded as the recording played. There it was all over again, Benjamin Caxton's speech. I was being dragged down that horrid path again. The whole visual of yesterday afternoon was back in my head. I remembered all too well, what Caxton was saying right before he was shot. As his words fell into a climactic pause, there was silence and then there was chaos."

Matthew looked up at me and asked, "You say you didn't hear any gun shot?"

"Nothing at all."

He looked to Sandra for reassurance and she confirmed my story by nodding.

"You didn't hear anything on the recording," I assured, "the waveform didn't reveal anything."

"Correct. There is no signal at that point, but your recorder is equipped with *noise cancellation technology*. It would cancel out the sound decibels of a gun shot."

"Why would it do that?"

"The gun the police are describing registers about 155 decibels a shot. What would happen if you were monitoring your recording with ear phones and you didn't have the effect of noise cancellation?"

I cringed and noticed Sandra did the same. Reaching onto the tabletop, I wrapped my hand around a container of coffee, seeking some comfort from the warm beverage. Matthew stood and began pacing slightly. He leaned against the metal shelving and fell into a pensive stare.

"The weapon may tell us very little about who committed this crime. I'm looking at it from every angle possible to try and find a motive for his murder."

I took a long sip of coffee and said, "Someone had issues with him."

He looked at me for a second and replied, "You mean *problems*."

I was certain I was accurate in my statement and I stuck to it. "No, I mean *issues*."

"I think you mean *problems*."

"*Issues!*"

I realized I was in for it when he said, "You know, euphemisms only mask reality, they don't change it."

Shrugging my shoulders, I asked, "What's a *euphemism*?"

He turned suddenly toward the shelf and his eyes were scanning for that dictionary. His hands stumbled trying to pry it off the shelf and I shouted with my hands waving, "No, no! I get it, I get it. The way you used it in the sentence, I understand the meaning. Context clues."

It was late; I was tired and did not feel like ducking another flying dictionary. He went back to his leaning and thinking.

Snapping my fingers, I pointed at him and declared, "I've got it. It means a *mild* expression."

He nodded his head to let me know I was correct. I decided to ask him a question.

"And how do you prefer your reality?"

"Like the devil himself!"

Sandra and I exchanged glances, but he wasn't even looking at us.

"Game plan," Sandra stated insistently.

"I'm still contemplating. We have to do this in the morning before school. That's the best I can offer. Except that I detect a real local feeling about this man."

"How so," I asked.

"His words and actions. His talk of community and the clear need to protect and preserve it and then, the addressing of the police force. His mission, for us to interpret, is what? To kill local politicians, defame Little League Baseball? I don't know. I picture a guy who never left this town or even the house he grew up in."

I thought about it while packing up my laptop. He turned toward the photos still on display. I was glad we were wrapping it up. My eyes were ready to shut. I couldn't see that we got any further, especially with the shooter and his letter, but sometimes things seemed clearer after some sleep. I remembered last night when he mentioned hacking. I asked if he had something specific in mind.

"This letter in the paper changes everything. We may need to hack into something, but not now. I have an idea."

"Well what is it?"

"I'm not telling you."

"Okay, that's great. Anything else," I asked.

"*Go now*," he said softly.

Sandra drove me home.

Chapter 7

Sleep did help a bit. As I made my way to school, it occurred to me that I was not sure what to expect. Would the police be looking for me? Mr. C? Or, perhaps even the shooter spotted me with the camera and wanted me out of the picture? The questions fueled my anxiety. I was looking for Sandra when I got the feeling that something was different this morning. The sun soaked back lawn area behind the school building had a crowd of students huddled on it. I made my way toward them.

Stepping around the crowd, I leaned in close and examined the back door of Serling High School. There was a notice fixed to it from the Department of Health. **H1N1** it read in big letters next to a caption titled *details*. The news referred to it as swine flu, but the main thing that was sinking in was the fact that school was closed.

Sandra appeared behind me reading it as well.

"I guess we have an epidemic," she said.

Then another voice I knew all too well interjected.

"Sommers, I thought I told you to disinfect yourself before coming to school."

I turned suddenly and saw the always arrogant, self-proclaimed know it all of Serling High, Derrick Porter.

Before I could grasp what he had said, his no fail laugh track kicked in. An average of three followers always stood right behind him and laughed at anything he said.

I began to speak, but felt a hand on my shoulder. Sandra was stepping around me. She stood face-to-face with the smug senior.

"I've got the perfect remedy for that big-headed ego of yours," she said pointing over his shoulder. "Ante up, don't be shy."

The small gathering looked in the direction where she pointed. A number of cars were parked there.

"You get in that foreign mechanism that you shamefully put American rims on and get ready to be *blown* away."

Porter looked around nervously and asked, "Right here?"

She didn't budge, "No. I don't play for the cheap seats. Let's take it up to Union Street, off the line, here to the highway. Name the stakes."

I saddled up next to her. She was on a tear. This would be wild. Sandra's Mustang against Derrick Porter's, as he refers to it, *current* model. I was looking right at him. His pawns were expecting him to remain cool and he was doing the exact opposite. He wanted no part of this race, but I didn't think he was going to have a choice. School was closed! There was no *saved by the bell* this time for Mr. Porter.

"Enough!"

My head turned slightly and was surprised. The cool, but commanding voice came from Matthew Livingston. I didn't know he was around.

Sandra turned as well and demanded, "This has to be done!"

"Later, perhaps. I need you now."

She looked at him for a moment and then stuck a finger in Derrick Porter's face, "We'll finish this when you least expect it. So be ready," she said flatly.

It wasn't so much a warning as it was a threat! Derrick morphed back into his arrogant self as Sandra started to walk away. He let out a couple of cocky laughs with his buddies, but the fact of the matter was that she planned on racing him. I wanted to ride shotgun with her to see Derrick get shown up.

I joined Matthew and Sandra as they made their way in the direction of her car. Looking back at the gathering, I was amazed to realize, no one had moved. We were just informed that school was closed and nobody had budged. The same group that was always finding creative excuses for not coming to school couldn't seem to find a reason to leave when given a legitimate means to.

"What's up," she asked the Genius.

"I want to see the baseball field."

I really wasn't sure what he was up to but, the next thing I knew we were climbing into the Mustang.

It was a brief ride over to Singleton Baseball Field. Matthew was out of the car ahead of us. It was roughly 8:30 in the morning, so the field was virtually empty with the exception of a groundskeeper working in the outfield.

"I take it the stage was here," he said standing on the grass.

"Correct," I answered. I noticed he was looking at small depressions in the soil where the stage had been supported.

He got down on one knee and looked out across the field. A light breeze began to blow as he gazed out toward his right. He stood and began walking. With decisive strides, he headed to an opening in the cyclone chain fence that was just beyond the first baseline.

Sandra and I followed, increasing our pace to keep up with him. The crisp and well-maintained grass of the ball field gave way to undeveloped patches of dirt and shrubbery. Matthew was looking down and up as well as side-to-side. I was not crazy about hanging out over here. If Serling High School had swine flu, I wondered what was lurking in this brushwood.

Another breeze came along, a little stronger than the first. I turned and gazed out at the peacefulness of the ball field. The blades of grass were still moist with dew that reflected the rays of the early sun. The dirt in the infield appeared undisturbed and almost anxious for the excitement of a slide into second base. It hardly seemed possible that this ball field was a murder scene a few days prior.

The groundskeeper was sitting on a large riding mower. It was a silky black machine with brilliant yellow rims. I found myself staring at it for a moment.

"You think it came from here," Sandra asked him. Matthew pointed toward the baseball field and answered, "I'm positive it didn't come from over there!"

The hum of an engine cut through the morning air. The slight breeze carried its dull rumbling.

"I'm not quoting trajectory or anything, I'm sure the police have that all mapped out. I just think..." Matthew paused suddenly.

"We're not positive they have it," Sandra offered. "You figure the news would be reporting it today and I've heard nothing of the sort."

The man was gripping the ample steering wheel that was situated in the center of the vehicle. From a distance, it seemed to be stemming from the wide engine covering. "Perhaps they are just keeping it quiet."

Sandra was taking in the area. Matthew was also.

"You saw no activity around here," as Matthew motioned to the wooded area.

I realized he was talking to me. I answered, "No, I'm positive. Just people in front of the stage and Caxton on the stage."

The machine glided across the level field. As it came closer, I noticed the driver seated on top of it. He had long brown hair, hanging from beneath a baseball cap, which was blowing in the morning breeze. He wore blue jeans, construction boots, and a sweatshirt that was sporting some grass stains on it.

A conversation was taking place between Sandra and Matthew and I was half listening.

"I don't think it's going to rain," he proclaimed looking up at the sky and then down at the field.

He began to walk further into the area's undergrowth. Sandra followed.

I looked at the cyclone chain fence. The man was maneuvering the riding mower through an opening in it. The noise was growing louder. I wasn't sure what he was up to, but he was clearly off the ball field and now onto the coarse terrain.

Matthew was looking down again. Sandra caught up to him. The rider was now picking up speed.

"Hey," I shouted in the direction of the driver. I wasn't heard. The noise from the machine was too loud. I began to walk in his direction. Jerking the steering wheel harshly, the mower turned chaotically. He did it again and I could see an apparent anguish in his face. His teeth were grinding as he yanked at the wheel. The mower rocked a bit on the uneven surface and the man gripped the wheel even tighter. Okay so much for a warning, now he was aiming right for me.

I ran toward the fence that had yellow sheets of paper taped to the posts. Reaching it, I placed my back against it. If he was going to hit me, he would end up crashing as well. He swerved towards me, dangerously close and made a wide u-turn. I stayed put. He was parallel with the fence coming for me. He would surely clip me now, so I ran. Not too smart on my part, he chased me right into the clearing.

The mower's speed increased and I began to wonder how much it was going to hurt when he caught up to me. I began to zigzag, left to right, forcing him to change direction. I looked over my shoulder and he was mercilessly making the contraption react in ways it probably wasn't designed to.

That was when my foot landed in a small hole. Tripping, I landed on one of those yellow sheets of paper. In big letters it read CONTACT CRIMESTOPPERS IF YOU HAVE…..I didn't have time to finish reading. I could hear the engine feverishly fighting against the landscape.

Something tugged at my denim jacket and I felt Sandra desperately trying to yank me off the ground. I thrust my body in the direction that she was pulling me. Getting to my feet, I noticed this maniac about five feet away. Too close for comfort! Sweat was racing down my back as I ran following Sandra. I looked to my right to see

Matthew Livingston crouched on one knee feeling for something in the tall weeds. He actually looked oblivious to the whole attack.

Sandra threw her arm out, preventing me from going further. My body feebly stopped. She turned and faced our pursuer. We had gained some ground on him, but he still seemed intent on running us down. He fed the machine gas and its engine raced. He was picking up speed!

"What are you doing," I shouted at her.

"Relax," was her response, eyeing the slick black machinery.

There was no exaggerated poise this time. Turning slightly, her back bent forward and both hands went flat, right on the hood of the approaching mower. Not as graceful as yesterday in the auditorium, but I didn't exactly see any judges on the sidelines. Her feet went straight up and she catapulted over the driver, landing directly behind him. The driver's face had an expression of disbelief mixed with anger. Yes, it was impressive. Stupidly as I watched her, the machine was *still* heading right for me.

Something was different however. The engine was whining and the vehicle had slowed considerably. The driver became manic, looking around the console, fumbling with something. He looked up at me. His jaw dropped and his vehicle stopped. His eyes continued to hunt around the console for the mechanical culprit that had caused his mower to seize.

I glanced behind him and Sandra was clutching something in her hand. It was a key on a large key ring.

The driver looked around confused. He looked at me, looked at Sandra behind him, and then looked down frustratingly at the vehicle beneath him.

"People," a voice called out. It was Livingston. His right hand held high, clutching a piece of rusted steel. "Is anyone else finding this metal around?"

The man turned, staring at Sandra he shouted, "Give that back!"

"Sure," she replied firing it at him. The key spiraled quickly in the air and caught him right in his large forehead. Bouncing off him, it landed on the ground below.

I sprinted to the rear of the mower and positioned myself next to her. Sandra grabbed him by the back of his sweatshirt and I did the same. We pulled him from behind, clear off the seat of his defunct vehicle and let him drop hard. I figured his age to be about twenty or twenty-one. He was lean and had a large cranium. I didn't care how old he was, I was furious. Besides, there were three of us he would have to contend with. Sandra and I stood close glaring down at him.

"You have some explaining to do and fast," she barked. The demand was accompanied by a sharp kick to his rib cage.

He twisted in reaction to it, clutching his side. He groaned in pain, but still didn't explain a thing.

Matthew had joined us, clutching three rusty pieces of steel.

"Did you two happen to see anything like this," he asked opening his hand to display the thick shards.

"We were a little busy," I replied still trying to catch my breath while delivering a kick of my own to our assailant.

"Why were you trying to run us over," Sandra demanded, her right foot raised to fire away again.

Matthew produced a plastic bag from his jacket pocket and dropped the items into it. Placing the bag back into the same pocket he looked down at the prone figure.

"Bring him over there," he said softly pointing toward the cluster of trees not far from us. "I don't want to be out in the open like this."

Sandra grabbed an ankle and I followed her lead, grabbing the other. We dragged him about forty feet to where the heart of the wooded area began. Matthew followed behind.

A tree with a wide trunk loomed high in front of us. Letting go of the ankles, we grabbed him by the back of his sweatshirt and spun him around. I looked at Sandra and she must have read my mind.

Clutching his sweatshirt, we lifted him partially and slammed his back into the mighty oak.

I was on one side of him and Sandra the other. We did not intend to let him up until we had some answers. He glared at both of us defiantly and then stared straight ahead at the methodically approaching figure. The matching slacks, shoes, and jacket were still meticulous. Even our prisoner seemed a bit freaked out.

Matthew stopped a few feet in front of the man whose legs were coiling inward as if they would provide protection in case he was kicked again.

"We've never met. My fault. I don't get out much."

His voice was decisive with his eyes cast upward, away from his prey. The treetops cast a shadow across his face.

"That doesn't mean I don't know a thing about you. For instance you're twenty years old, left-handed, employed as a landscaper, and you are a high school drop out."

His body cowered against the tree. He gazed up at Livingston with a terrified look on his face.

"Who told you all that?"

"Your right hand is the one that is significantly bruised and cut because it lacks dexterity. Although in your line of work, you use both hands equally. The boots you wear, they were discontinued four years ago and you have gotten approximately four years of labor out of them. Judging by the boot size it places you in your mid-teens when you acquired them. The condition of… you know let us just get to the point. Why were you trying to run over these two individuals?"

The man looked anxious like he was going to try to make a break for it. He looked at Sandra who clenched a fist in anticipation and he calmed himself.

Matthew was unfazed by the man's reluctance to speak. He continued, "You maintain the grounds at Singleton Baseball Field, correct?"

The man shrugged as a sign of agreement.

The stare stayed in place, but Matt's left hand raised and he pointed outward. "That my friend is over there!" Pointing at the ground he asked, "Why are you driving that device over here?"

"Someone asked me to."

All eyes were upon him as he broke his silence.

"I was getting ready to trim the outfield and this guy came over to me. Guessed he was the owner of the grounds or something. Said he needed some sort of favor. Asked if I could do a once over in the surrounding area. Said an investor was coming to look at the whole place."

"Anything else," Matt asked cocking his head to the left.

For a minute, I thought the vow of silence was renewed, but then he spoke. "Gave me fifty bucks to do it quick."

"Whoa," Sandra and I exclaimed in unison.

I thought for a second and then asked, "Did the fifty include running us over?"

He looked up at me and answered, "No. Sorry 'bout that. I just don't like people."

Sandra looked skyward and just whistled.

Glancing at Livingston he said, "That's one of the reasons I left high school."

"You're about to get a reprieve," Matt said, his eyes fixed on the neighboring ball field. "Describe this gentleman who gave you fifty dollars."

He sat up a little bit more relaxed. "He had shades on, the mirrored kind. Wore a hat too."

"Kind of like a guy trying to hide something," Matt asked.

"Yeah, I guess. He was old, maybe in his early fifties. Wore a black jacket, covered him pretty good. Honestly, couldn't tell you more than that."

"And he just wanted you to run the mower over the field?"

"Yep. For fifty bucks."

Matt had his arms folded across his chest. "Okay, that's all I need to know. *Go now!*"

Looking relieved not to have to deal with people any longer, the groundskeeper picked himself up and walked between Matt and myself in the direction of his riding mower.

Sandra asked, "Do you think he wanted the area disrupted for some reason?"

"Yes. He might just be acting cautiously, making sure he didn't leave anything behind. But, how cautious is taking a chance of revealing his identity?"

I chimed in, "About as cautious as writing that letter the newspaper printed."

"Either way," he said, "it's risky. First things first." He pulled out the plastic bag from his pocket. "I need to examine these. Secondly, we need to find out just who owns this property. Town Hall should have the public records on anything in this community. Could you two look into that for me?"

"Sure," Sandra answered. "We'll drop you off and then head over there."

The three of us made our way back toward the street. Reaching the edge of the grounds, I noticed something stuck to my right sneaker. It was one of those yellow papers. Snatching it up, I read the crime stoppers message. Yep, any information about the Caxton shooting, guess who they wanted you to call. Withers and Riley. I crumbled up the paper and dropped it in a tall, blue metal trashcan by the curb. We got in the car.

CHAPTER 8

AT 9:30, AFTER WE dispatched the Genius, Sandra and I were seated at a wooden table in Town Hall. The building shared offices with the Chamber of Commerce. I knew the Chamber was responsible for protecting and promoting the business interests of merchants. Town Hall was where I was in the gray area. It looked a little like a museum, with large sections of glass enclosures displaying old photographs. On the table where we were seated were three computers.

Sandra got the attention of a young woman who worked there. She logged us onto the computer and it immediately displayed a map of the town. The map was linked by section to the Town's *Geographical Information System*, which displayed all public documents and information.

I found it interesting as I explored our community. Public property was pretty much an open page. Singleton Baseball Field belonged to the town. The property to the immediate west of it was the subject of public hearings for annexation. Three hearings to be exact. It listed the current owner as Wilson James McMillan, age fifty-seven. It indicated an estimated property value and a yearly tax that the town had assessed.

I navigated away from the site after making an account in my notebook. I got curious. The homepage on the Town Hall computer had an icon for appendicies. I clicked on it and typed Wilson James

McMillan into the search area. It referenced a few articles in the *Village Gate*, our community's weekly newspaper. I jotted down the dates and logged off the computer.

The lady who set us up at the computer was standing behind a desk with a registry book in the center of it. Her fingers were gliding along line after line. She had gum that she was cracking in her mouth like clockwork. *Crack. Crack. Crack.* There was some other awful noise emanating from her as well. Looking down, I noticed her grinding the plastic heel of one of her shoes into the carpet. It was making a plastic *squeaking* noise that accompanied the sound of cracking gum. She noticed me and smiled.

"Yes, what else can I help you with?"

I was going to suggest for starters that she stop making the annoying or should I say, vexing noises, but I needed her assistance.

"Do you have archives of the *Village Gate*?"

"Yes we do," *Crack! Crack!* "Right down there in those large binders on the shelf. They are sorted by date." *Crack. Crack. Crack.*

I turned and there were three aisles with reference books and materials on the shelves. I told Sandra the most recent date and we began searching. The spine of the big binders denoted a starting and closing month and year.

"Here we go," Sandra said pulling one of the binders off the shelf. She had the most recent date that referenced Mr. McMillan in her hand.

Opening the binders we noticed the inserts were in protective plastic with copies of each page of the *Village Gate* inside of them. There wasn't a whole lot of news in this particular issue, but it did contain a black and white photo. It was a committee for the town's historical society and in the center of it was a man in his fifties wearing mirrored shades and a black hat.

I pointed at the picture and asked in a low voice, "Does this guy look like someone we should know?"

"Yeah it does," Sandra whispered back. "I'll run off a copy so we can show the Genius. There's a machine up front."

I felt defeated. It only added some credibility to the story we were told over at Singleton Field. Perhaps an investor was coming to look at the area. I had hitched my hopes onto the thought that our shooter had returned to the crime scene, but then again that would be just crazy. I waited for Sandra to return the insert and I placed the binder back on the shelf.

The scene in the loft had changed a little. Matthew sat on the yellow sofa. His microscope was on the wheeltop and he was perched over it. One of the rusted shards he found next to the baseball field was being examined.

I sat in the folding chair opposite him and opened my notebook. I glanced over what I had written when I noticed Matthew look up from the microscope and lean back.

Sandra who was standing behind me asked, "Okay, what's so interesting about those pieces of steel?"

"I became interested in the unusual shape of them. Rough and rounded all except for one area where it is fine and smooth."

He held the piece that he was examining and remarked, "Its metal from a train rail. The fine side is the result of friction caused by the actual wheels of a train."

He stood up and walked to the rear of the loft. "I have some books that belonged to my grandfather, pictorial histories of this town."

He came back to the sofa and sat. On the wheeltop next to the microscope, he placed three old books. They were in relatively good condition. Each had a tight binding, hardly any creasing, and very little yellowing on the pages. He picked up the one on top and flipped through it.

"This is the most recent of the three. It was published twenty-five years ago. It contains maps dating back a hundred years ago. Some of the street names are different, but it does mention what the names were changed to."

Sandra and I sat on each side of him as he opened the book. On one page were a few black and white photos and on the other a map explaining the location where the photos were taken.

"Look at the map," Matthew said pointing to it. It outlined an area in town and showed the railroad going through it.

Pointing a little to the left of it he said, "This is Sutton Field, which is now the area next to the baseball field."

"But the train doesn't run through there," I remarked.

"Correct, it runs a little bit south of it. Read this paragraph."

He pointed to it and I read aloud, "As of 1917, Sutton Field became an access point for steam engines. It housed the town's only coal yard where trains making long journeys east and west could refuel."

"The train tracks were moved in the late 1920s," he explained. "The steam engine declined in the mid 1930s and made way for the diesel-electric locomotives. No more coal."

"Your point?"

He stood and looked at my pictures still on display. He was pointing to the picture of the stage. It was then that I noticed he had placed them in some sort of order, almost reconstructing the scene. Below the photo of the stage were pictures of the audience standing on the grass. Then a picture that displayed some of the wooded area that I had just learned was once called Sutton Field, was beneath that, followed by the rest.

"You see what I see Dennis."

"Yes, the stage, the podium, the crime scene. I see. I see."

Sandra joined us as Matthew pointed away.

"Here is Caxton," his hand pointed to the picture of the stage and then shifted to the right to the picture of the rural area. "The shot came from this direction. No shooter is seen. Do you think he had wings?"

I wasn't sure if he was serious, so I shook my head *no*.

"So we're fairly certain he didn't fly away. Then perhaps he went down, concealed himself somehow. The police have no reports or sightings of anyone in the woods. Where is this man?"

I didn't grasp it all or any of it for that matter, but felt I had to contribute something. So I reported what I did know based on my investigation.

"The owner of the property in question is a Mr. Wilson James McMillan. Sandra and I found a picture of him in the local paper from about a year ago. Fits the description that the groundskeeper gave us."

Handing him the photocopy, he glanced at it for a second and handed it back to me. He focused on the pictures again and tapped on the one that showed some of the wooded area. "We must go back. There's something more to this!" Grabbing a duffel bag that I noticed held some tools in it, he lead the way out of the loft. Sandra and I said nothing as we followed.

Chapter 9

AND BACK WE WENT. Through the grounds and deep into the area that Matthew pinpointed as a hiding spot for the shooter. Sometimes I wish he was wrong, just to prove that he was human. But, after some odd minutes of poking and prodding at nature, he found what he was looking for. Brown grass had completely covered it. Three trees surrounded it. I realized that *Johnny Antisocial*, who we had met earlier, or anyone else for that matter would never get a riding lawn mower across it.

Dropping the duffel bag, Matthew kneeled and placed his hands into the soil beneath the dead grass. His jaw muscles tightened slightly and the next thing I knew something was being raised. Looking closer I realized grass and vines had been covering a wooden lid of some sort. Sandra and I immediately went to assist him and together we managed to open it completely. Smooth soil and a slight indentation on the edge of the earth indicated that it had been lifted before. Recently!

Matthew stood up at the edge of the opening. I looked around quickly to see if we were being observed. We weren't. Matthew removed a flashlight from the duffel bag and shined it below. I stood a few feet behind him, almost afraid to peer inside. Sandra waited anxiously behind me.

The light still shined below as his head turned toward us. His voice was confident yet cryptic when he said, "This is where the shooter hid."

It was an incredible discovery and I envied his intuition. While I realized the path of our investigation had become less overgrown, it was still rock-strewn and dangerous. The area Matthew was shining his light on reminded me of a grave. A little bigger perhaps, but narrow all the same. I didn't want to enter it, but as a reporter I knew I had to. I at least felt compelled to.

"No chance he dropped his check book down there," Sandra asked.

Removing a decent sized rope from the duffel bag the Genius replied, "We're going to find out."

"Cool," she said and smiled.

"Exactly what is cool about this," I asked her hearing the desperation in my own voice. "Maybe there's a snake down there, some racoons, perhaps even a bear. What's cool about that?"

Matthew was tying the rope around one of the trees close by. He placed his foot against the trunk of the tree. Gripping the rope he pushed off testing the durability of the knot that he had just tied.

"Well they didn't kill our shooter if he lived to write that letter," she argued.

"Or maybe he killed it," Matt added inching closer to the edge of the opening. He crouched down and I could guess the drop to be about seven feet deep. He grabbed his duffel bag, lowered it into the hole and let it drop.

Looking at Sandra he said, "I need you to stay up here and make sure that rope stays tied. Dennis and I will go down and have a look."

"Whoa," I protested. "I'm fairly confident that I can make sure the rope doesn't become untied. Besides, I don't think I passed the rope climb in gym class. That makes me unqualified."

He was disappearing from sight as he descended. Hearing his feet hit the ground, I realized he wasn't going to ask twice.

"To quote the Genius," Sandra said, "you must go now!" She

pointed to the rope and I slowly picked it up. Yeah, I had to go alright. I heard Livingston's voice echo from below. It painted a creeped out image.

"It's only about eight feet to the bottom."

"Yeah," I shouted down, "and your average grave is about six."

Sandra placed her hand firmly on my shoulder and said, "Nothing is going to happen. I'll be standing here the whole time."

Trusting her, I lifted the rope and wrapped it around my palms.

"Don't let it fully extend," she said, "or you'll hit the bottom fast."

I wound up a few feet and started to descend. My sneakers were hitting the wall of earth in front of me, securing my position, but I had gotten a bit heavier since the last time I relied upon a rope for support. It wasn't bad once I was halfway down. Although at some point, I was going to have to climb up. My feet hit the dirt and I immediately felt cooler.

"Careful," he called shining the flashlight at my feet. "Don't move."

My mind raced into panic mode for I could think of nothing else but snakes. I relaxed when I realized he was referring to the soil. With my feet spread about two feet apart I noticed something between them. It was a powdery substance, darker than the soil. Matthew had the flashlight above it.

"I don't claim to know a whole lot about firearms, but I believe its gun powder."

"Not cigarette ashes," I asked, remaining still and surprised by my ability to think rationally in this pit.

"This isn't the place to find out," he remarked taking a small, plastic ziplock bag from his coat pocket. "I have a lab for getting answers to these types of questions."

He was lying on his stomach with the plastic bag next to the powdery substance. Resting the flashlight on the ground, he took out a pen and used it to push the matter into the bag. Sealing it shut he placed it in his coat pocket and retrieved the flashlight.

"Can I move now?"

"Yes you can," he answered shining the light further down the tunnel like surroundings.

"I think this was done recently."

"What do you mean," I asked.

"That cover that I lifted must have been a hatchway for coal storage a long time ago. I can only assume that the storage area was the sum of the distance of all the lengths and sides of the object, namely that hatchway."

I stared at him for a second and said, "We go to the same high school. Whatever they're teaching you, they certainly aren't teaching me. So would you mind explaining what you just said to me very slowly. And feel free to add diagrams, a video, whatever you think might assist my thought process."

"Essentially the area we are standing in shouldn't be wider than the hatch above."

Spinning around, he shined the flashlight on the narrow corridor that extended deeper in front of us.

"Someone did some tunneling, and recently," he said.

I understood now. Someone found this hole in the ground and created a passageway out of it. Livingston was already making his way down the makeshift path. We had pretty much lost the sunlight from the open hatch. He stopped and reached his hands to the walls on each side. There were only a few inches on each side of him.

"We can assume he's not any wider than this," he declared and continued walking. The flashlight was shining except there was nothing but dirt to be seen in the shadows. We traveled about twenty feet and the path angled to the right. So we made a right turn as well.

It was a similar corridor in height and width and extended between ten and twenty feet. Livingston continued slowly, shining the light all around, he followed the tunnel to its end. There was something above him and it was not more dirt. He flashed a beam of light on what appeared to be a square section of wood paneling.

"I have to reach that," he said pointing to the wood panel above our heads.

"Okay," I agreed, unsure of how he intended to do this.

His eyes looked up and down and then settled on me.

"Kneel down; I am going to stand on your back," as he handed me the flashlight.

I was not surprised. I refused to argue. Planting my knees in the dark soil, I leaned forward. He placed a foot just below my shoulder blades. Steadying himself, he placed his other foot next to it. In a second, he was balancing courtesy of my back. I could tell his hands were beneath the paneling. I could hear him banging on it. A few good hits released it and we were suddenly being bathed in sunlight.

I felt his weight released from my back so I looked upward. Getting his forearms above ground, he began to pull himself up. I got to my feet and brushed dirt from my pants. That was when I heard a high pitch sound whistle by and Matthew Livingston fell on top of me. We both hit the soil, hard! Rolling over, I could see his eyes open wide.

With an unusually higher pitch to his voice he announced, "That was a gunshot!"

My cell phone was vibrating and looking at the caller ID I could tell it was Sandra. I couldn't make out much of the wailing, but I understood two words, STAY DOWN!

I started to crawl back rapidly in the direction from where we had entered.

"Is that Sandra," Matthew was shouting at me.

"Yeah," I shouted back.

"What does she see?"

I relayed the question and she told me that she saw no one. It sounded like she was running.

"Nothing," I said frantically, "She sees nothing."

I had a bad feeling, as if I was a prop in a carnival shooting gallery. "We're sitting ducks," I called out. The phone disconnected.

"Stay put," he said looking around.

I looked at our confines and thought that maybe this would be a grave after all. I heard noise above. It sounded like machinery. A shadow passed over the opening. I could not make out what it was. My cell phone went off again.

"Yeah Sandra," I said, frightened.

Her voice was calm, "Climb up and stay low to the ground when you crawl out. Trust me. Just do it!"

I turned around and relayed the message to Livingston. He had no problem with that and told me to start climbing. I had one problem with that. I didn't think I could.

He walked up to the wall of dirt and said, "Ignore the rope." Squatting down, he told me to step on his shoulders and balance myself against the wall. I placed one foot on a shoulder, got my balance and then scaled up on the other.

"Okay," he said, "you're not that far from the top. I'm going to stand up as much as I can. When you're elevated high enough, get your arms out and pull yourself out the best you can."

I didn't have time to think about it because he was lifting me upwards. He had a strong back because in a couple of seconds I was high enough to get my elbows out. I started to climb out and felt him pushing me from under my feet. It helped.

Escaping, I crawled on my stomach while looking around. The first thing I saw, about fifteen feet away was the Mustang. Sandra drove it as close as she could get to us. The car did not fit between the tall oak trees that now looked somewhat menacing with their leaves swaying in a dull grayish green blur. Looking at the hole in the ground, I noticed just past it a large metal garbage can lying on its side. It had the potential to serve as a barricade, shielding us as we exited. I remembered Sandra's command to stay low. Whoever was shooting could not hit us with that metal container in the way at least I hoped. Whatever it was, it was sharp thinking on her part. I saw her crouched low by the car and I could see the trunk open. She must have driven the garbage can over here.

In less than a minute, I saw Matthew Livingston climb out via the rope. He looked around as well. Clearly noticing the garbage can, he crawled swiftly in my direction.

"Let's go," Sandra called, still crouched by the car.

"We have got to cover these openings," Matt replied, jerking his thumb in the direction of the ditch we had just climbed out of.

I knew he was crazy, but we couldn't win with him. He would stay there and risk being shot at unless we covered the holes. The air was silent.

"Quickly," Sandra called out as she ran in a crouching position toward the hole.

Surrounding the wooden lid, we each grabbed a corner of it and slid it towards the opening in the ground. It landed in its familiar setting. Again, it looked like part of the landscape, camouflaged perfectly. Still crouching low, we all grabbed the metal can and moved forward, keeping it in front of us the whole time as protection. We were careful not to fall into the second hole that we had just discovered. There was a thick square of wood heavily covered in ivy and vines. It was the one Matt had knocked loose. Placing the can in front of the hole, we picked up the wood and covered it, while protecting our hides. Keeping low, we dashed to the Mustang. Thankfully the shooting had stopped. Sandra drove speedily off the property. Fitting her car tightly between an opening in the fencing, we reached the main street and got out of there, *alive*!

Chapter 10

I do not recall discussing a particular destination, but we arrived at the loft. Matthew led the way. The determination in his stride was unmistakable as he approached the garage and stopped firmly.

Standing behind him, I could see he was examining a white envelope. It had been affixed to the door by a thumbtack when we arrived. Delicately handling everything, he freed the envelope and removed the contents which appeared to be a letter. Unfolding it, he stared for a very unsettling minute.

"What now," asked Sandra. Her voice was wary.

He held it up so we could see. There were very few words on it. I found myself reading aloud.

"STAY AWAY! I know how to find you. You'll NEVER find me!"

My knees almost buckled as a chill raced past them on the way up my spine. No one was speaking, so I elected myself.

"What's this all about," my voice got high with excitement. "Do we have targets on our backs?"

Matt was carefully refolding the paper. "I don't think it was my back he was shooting at this afternoon."

His words resounded icily. Unlocking the garage door, we made our way up to the loft. Sandra and I took seats, while Matthew remained standing. His hands were joined behind his back as his head leaned forward to take in the pictures still on display.

"Fat lot of good those did," I called out. "You found the hiding spot but…"

"We got him to reappear," he interrupted me. "In many ways we found him."

He quickly started taking the photos down. He was dropping them in a pile. The last picture was the one I took of Sandra. He handed it to her.

"Thanks," she said sarcastically, "hopefully they won't be using it for an obituary."

Her words were grim. A feeling of eminent danger was infiltrating our space.

"Not on my watch," Matt said, turning to face us.

Perhaps it was the consuming fear that got a hold of me, but I jumped up off the couch.

"Hey," I shouted, "some whacko killed somebody and now apparently we've gotten under his skin. I'm a tad bit worried. This guy is certifiable! He kills a politician and writes letters to the newspaper practically bragging about it. Maybe we should dig up Sigmund Freud to get inside the shooter's head. Talk about insanity! You were just shot at and all you did was find some hole in the ground…"

"Exactly!"

His words were firm and so was the finger he was pointing at me. Wait a second, did I just figure something out?

Matthew elaborated.

"I wanted to find out how he concealed himself when he shot Benjamin Caxton. Once I found out, I wanted to advertise it. I wanted to call everyone. The cops. The press. Caxton's campaign office. I wanted him to know he was discovered. Turns out I didn't have to."

"Nice," Sandra smiled knowingly.

I did not understand the logic behind it. Thankfully, he continued as my heart gradually reverted to its regular rhythm.

"This guy can't handle exposure. He loves the mystery. He is a person who is hidden, yet sends letters that will not be traced. He's too confident that he won't be caught. He's arrogant! He taunts the police over the fact that they will not find him. Yet, we just did something he did not want anyone to do. We found out something about him! He built up a head of steam only to be derailed."

"Loving it," Sandra commented, still smiling.

"So the question remains. Was it Wilson James McMillan, at Singleton Baseball Field, who paid cro-magnon man fifty bucks to disrupt the crime scene?"

"McMillan is the shooter," Sandra sounding puzzled.

"No. I did say I believe the shooter is a local resident. He could have easily read the same town paper you read that had the picture of McMillan in it."

Snapping her fingers, Sandra exclaimed, "Impersonation, the shades, black hat and all."

"Pretty intense fellow to go to those lengths, wouldn't you say?"

Sandra replied, "Indeed, and he was keeping an eye on something over there today. Think he forgot something?"

Matthew sat on the sofa. Raising the ziplock bag, with the dark powder, he said, "Perhaps. I think I found some gunpowder down there. Maybe he was checking for that. Either way he showed himself."

Confusion was weighing on me. Not being in school, I had lost track of time. Even though I felt displaced, I needed to contribute something. Rubbing my rope burned hands I offered, "Is there anything I can do to help?"

He got up quickly and walked to the rear of the loft. I could hear him grabbing something off the shelf. When he returned, he held a tattered notebook and a sharpened pencil.

"When can you get to the library," he asked me.

I shrugged my shoulders and replied, "I can go tonight."

He began writing in the notebook. "When I mentioned *hacking* the other day, I wanted to know if you could *hack* into their main server."

I leaned back on the sofa and for the first time in a long while, I smiled. Finally, *they* needed something that required *my* skills. I thought about how I wanted to answer the question and then placed my hands behind my head. Depositing my feet on the wheel top I announced, "Yes, I can."

Matthew tore the piece of paper out of the notebook and folded it. Handing it to me he said, "This is a list of things on my mind."

He made another trip to the rear of the loft, this time returning with his microscope. He gently placed it on the wheel top. Gazing at the envelope he said, "I need to see if our friend left any of himself on this letter, as well as checking into that powder."

Sandra stood and said, "I need to get to work. Need me to check in later?"

"No," Matt replied. "If school is open tomorrow, I'll see you there."

I got up also and looked at him adjusting his microscope. He was in that weird zone again.

"Any advice," I pressed.

He raised his eyes from the microscope with a look of irritation combined with agitation.

"*Go now,*" he said, "and don't be so predictable in the route you take there!"

Despite all of the morning's happenings, it was the first appearance of human emotion I had sensed all day.

CHAPTER 11

OUR PUBLIC LIBRARY WAS open this evening until 8 o'clock. Heading over at a 6:45 gave me a better part of an hour to work with. Feeling a bit like a thief in the night with my tools, I placed my laptop on a table in the rear and my bag of tricks underneath it. It was not a terribly crowded night, so I would need only a little cover and concealment while I worked. A school textbook, my binder, and a large encyclopedia surrounded my setup and I pretended to be consumed with all of them.

Now don't get me wrong, when it comes to hacking I'm not part of some community that does this. It is merely something that comes easy to me, and not much else does. When I made the comparison to a thief in the night, that's not entirely true. I am more of a home computer hobbyist. For some strange reason, I identify with the unusual alphabet of computer infiltration.

The town library has a web site. Who doesn't these days? I used a software application called *Port Scanner,* which probed the library network for open ports.

SCORE!

They did not even have a firewall. I guess they save a lot of money on the assumption that no one would want to hack into the library's server. I could see everything. Removing Matthew's list from my pocket, I examined it.

At first, it seemed bizarre. I felt like I was in American history class. The top of the list directed me to all inquiries about former President John F. Kennedy. Well he was right; Kennedy was like a rash all over the library search engines. I looked up at the six computer terminals that were all in constant use and estimated about how many people used them a day. Looking back at my laptop, I saw a huge number of searches occurred over the course of an hour, three weeks ago. Wow! I couldn't hook up any externals to copy the information without looking suspicious, so I made notes in my book. I filled up three pages on this category of searches about JFK and particularly the details surrounding his assassination. I wasn't sure what a *knoll* was, but the word kept popping up, connected to the former President.

Once I copied all of that, I moved onto the next subject on the list. Psychological Serial Killers. Whoa! There were volumes of searches on maniacs who killed and left specific calling cards. One article was titled *Modus Operandi*, which I learned was a Latin phrase meaning *Method of Operating*. Now I could see the purpose of these searches. The Caxton killer must have been developing his own *Modus Operandi. Or was it his own?* He seemed to be borrowing bits and pieces of documented cases, but too vast to make a connection between them.

It was almost 8 when I finished jotting all the information down. They were announcing the library's closing in fifteen minutes so I turned off my computer and collected my things. I left as inconspicuously as I had entered. There was a lot of information rolling around in my head. Making my way towards home, it was only a few minutes before I rounded Brenner Lane. I noticed the unmarked police car on the opposite side of the street. I picked up my pace, realizing I should have taken a less predictable route home. Figuring it was my good friends Withers and Riley I knew they wouldn't get out of the car and pursue me. I figured right. They started the car and pulled about twenty feet in front of me and then got out.

You can probably guess what I'm going to tell you next. The

suits? Yes, the suits with the exception of the color were identical. Anyway they approached me with their neverending quest to seem intimidating.

"Funny guy," Withers spoke, "mind telling us what you did with the card for that camera?"

Finally. I had practiced my alibi since Monday when they had taken the camera. Why so long to notice the missing card?

"What are you talking about," I asked looking completely confused.

"Don't get cute," Riley whined, "you were seen taking pictures. When we vouchered the camera, the card was mysteriously missing."

I looked at him and acted shocked by his statement. "It sounds to me like you lost the memory card for my school's digital camera."

Riley asked, "Is your freaky friend playing amateur detective again by withholding evidence?"

Remembering that Matt had discarded the pictures, I replied, "I can't say. Why don't you ask him. What I can say is Mr. C from the school newspaper will be contacting you about replacing that card. Will it be coming out of the Withers and Riley retirement fund?"

They were searching for a comeback. I wanted to continue with my act, but remembered all the notes that were in my bag. I couldn't afford for them to start poking around. I said goodnight and went home.

I ate a late dinner and caught up with my folks. After taking the garbage out, I grabbed the notebook and made a visit to the loft.

The microscope was placed in the center of the wheel top along with the envelope. His right foot was on the edge of the makeshift table. Sitting opposite him, I was able to take in the whole picture. When I had left earlier, he was examining the envelope. Now he appeared stalled.

"Any luck," I asked nodding at the envelope.

"I found some traces of polymer microparticles."

"Okay. Is that good?"

"It means he was wearing latex gloves. I didn't examine the powder yet, I had to make some phone calls. How did you do?"

I started to read aloud from the notebook. His eyes were shut, but I knew he was absorbing it all. It took awhile and when I finally finished he seemed satisfied. Now, I had a few questions for him.

"The things you listed on that note. How did you know someone would be looking up information on those things specifically?"

His foot remained on the edge of the wheel top with his hands grasping his right knee. "Every aspect of this murder is completely unoriginal. The letters he sent, the language, style, and purpose has been done before. The man is a copycat killer!"

The chills I experienced earlier returned. I thought about what he had just said and decided to ask another question. "Everybody has a computer. How did you know this guy went to the library to use one?"

"You should remember when we discovered that cult not too long ago. You probed the girl's computer for all the data we needed. Fortunately for us, she used her home computer. This guy did extensive research on those subjects. Given his desire to remain anonymous, he couldn't risk leaving a trail of searches like that on his home computer. While I was listening to the recording of Caxton's speech, he referenced the library and their computers. Subscribing to my theory that the shooter is a resident, it made sense to me. Research is done in a library and that's exactly where he did his. Perhaps it's a message from Caxton himself. Find his killer!"

Looking at him he appeared unphased. It was a major discovery, but he wasn't dwelling on it. Like an extreme strategist, he appeared to be planning his next move. He stood up.

"A copycat," his words were soft, "what does that mean to you?"

Shrugging my shoulders I guessed, "He lives vicariously through the acts of others to the point where he reenacts them."

Now his hand grasped his chin tightly, as his eyes fell upon me. "A very credible hypothesis."

"So that's the whole story?"

"No, it means he's going to kill again!"

As his voice dissolved, I wondered if I was to be that next so called statistic. Maybe Sandra or even the Genius himself.

"When," I demanded.

"We have to look at a number of possibilities. Timelines based on events in the past, after all he is a copycat. But then again there is the number one reason for him to kill again."

"Yes?"

"Opportunity! We can't afford to overlook that."

"When do you plan on looking at those possibilities?"

"School will be closed tomorrow. I already confirmed this. Thus, we have a very small window of opportunity to check all of this out."

I sensed he was going to tell me to go now, so I stood and said, "By the way, the wonder twins stopped me today."

He looked up at me and asked, "How'd it go?"

I bowed slowly and replied, "And the Oscar goes to…"

"Congratulations, *now go!*"

I left him with his thoughts.

CHAPTER 12

WHEREVER HE GOT HIS information from, Matt was right.

It was Thursday morning and school was closed. The word was that the infected area of the building had been properly sanitized and Serling High would reopen tomorrow.

It was good for me. I had a customer who wanted a full upgrade on his computer and I took care of it early. The cash I earned was decent and I enjoyed knowing my skills generated income. I hope one day my writing will do the same. Nevertheless, with that out of the way, I found myself walking home. Approaching the house, I realized I had never taken in the newspaper.

Reaching down to the bottom step, I grabbed it and it slipped right out of the plastic bag. Landing on the top step the paper unfolded, displaying the headline.

CAXTON KILLER TAUNTS

I felt a startling sharp sensation take hold of my body. My hands were shaking as my knees gave way slightly. Sitting down on the concrete step to steady myself, I picked up the morning edition. My eyes froze on the reproduction of a handwritten letter that consumed the front page. I could not decipher any hidden messages from it; in fact, I could not even read the whole thing. I leapt up and beat it to Baskerville Street.

Taking the steps to the loft two at a time, I reached the top and found Matthew standing there. My breathing had increased to a noticeable pant as I dropped the newspaper on the wheel top.

"I saw it," he said solemnly.

"What now," I asked with little self-control.

"It's another warning to back off."

"And that's because he noticed us, right?"

"Not necessarily. The police are looking for him, who knows where they have been. Perhaps they disrupted something."

I composed myself. I had felt that perhaps our actions caused this verbal threat. Now I realized that the police were actually doing a manhunt too and were most likely stirring things up, too.

Sitting on the sofa Matthew said, "Another development has arisen. The FBI is now involved. It has been on the news all morning. The press received that letter last night, printed it this morning, and now the public is demanding answers. The police along with the FBI are answering questions at Town Hall at three o'clock this afternoon."

I was a bit relieved. Maybe the police and the FBI converging on this person might get the target off my back. It was then I realized. In the eyes of Matthew Livingston, the shooter was the one with a target on his back.

"I will be occupied here today. I need you at Town Hall."

I looked around. The pictures were gone, his lab equipment was away, and there was nothing happening. Then again, if he claimed to be occupied, why argue?

"Okay," I conceded, "I'm there. What do I do?"

"You're a reporter. Take notes."

"Okay, how about I take notes?'

He was not amused.

"Don't give any information. When you are finished at Town Hall, check in with me."

When I left the loft, the only thing he was occupied with was the sofa. I grabbed my Blackberry and called Sandra. Filling her in, she offered to tag along. I never refuse that offer.

CHAPTER 13

AT A 2:45, WE were searching for a parking space. We ended up finding one about two blocks away. It appeared that Town Hall was a happening today.

When we entered, we were directed to a conference room that was filled with people talking in agitated tones. Some occupied metal folding chairs, while the rest just stood. Getting a glimpse of the front, I noticed a podium. I sure was seeing a lot of podiums this week.

A gentleman, who looked like he had gotten up on the wrong side of the bed this morning, as well as several mornings before today, approached the podium and the room quieted down immediately. Next to him was another man I had never seen before. Behind them were Withers, Riley, and the old supervisor from the precinct squad room.

The man speaking introduced himself as Special Agent Ryan from the FBI and in a firm uncompromising tone of voice gave a behavioral profile of the Caxton shooter. I assumed his reason for that was to quell the apprehension of the public gathered here today. The more information provided, however redundant, the more likely the masses would believe the authorities had a handle on the situation.

He spoke, "In the Bureau we have seen lots of cases like this before. By writing letters, they are given a sense of control. They are only…"

"What about us, the residents," a bleach blond man in his thirties called out. "What are we, human targets?"

"No," Agent Ryan responded. "Case in point, the shooter only took action one time."

Wrong my friend! I could not reveal how incorrect his information was. I remembered Matthew telling me not to give up any information. Perhaps this was his way of fishing for additional information.

I saw Mrs. Floyd in the crowd. I realized she must be concerned, having witnessed the Caxton shooting firsthand. I wondered if she was going to rifle through her nostrils again. She was with another woman who hollered at the agent, "What about when I take my kids to school? Are we safe?"

"You're perfectly safe. This individual wants to cause fear and is using these letters to do so."

I'm no psychology expert, but it seemed the agent was trying to get further and further away from the subject of Caxton's murder. He seemed focused on the letters.

Detective Riley stepped in front of Agent Ryan at the podium and said, "People, we came here today to explain the situation at hand. We don't want you to be alarmed…"

"Alarmed," an older woman with red hair shouted out, "I don't want to leave my house with this maniac on the loose!"

Riley continued, "Listen, you have to trust the amount of manpower that is going into this investigation. We are working around the clock to ensure this individual is caught. Your safety, as always, is our number one concern."

An old man in a long gray overcoat and black hat stepped to the front of the audience and with worn wrinkled hands, slammed his walking stick on the floor.

Pushing a pair of spectacles up his nose he asked angrily, "I thought you claimed you knew the suspect was of a military background."

Riley paused for a second and said, "We are looking extensively through military records. Unfortunately, these checks take some time and there are many records to examine. We still believe it is a strong possibility. The shooter was well-trained with firearms, the kind of training received in the military."

Another woman, apparently a parent asked, "What about our children, are they threatened?"

Agent Ryan replied coolly, "We are analyzing why the *one* and *only* victim was a political candidate. As far as we can tell, children are not a target in any way. We will answer just a few more questions. We must get back to our investigation."

While he said he was limiting the press conference to just a few more questions, Sandra and I found ourselves there for another half hour. Finally, the police concluded, without a conclusion. People were heading for the exit, disgruntled and still in a state of heightened anxiety, and we did the same.

Stepping outside, the bright afternoon sun caught me off guard. Having just spent the better part of the hour in Town Hall, my eyes needed a little adjusting. The crowd was scattering and the street emptied quickly. There seemed to be an unwillingness to linger outdoors in view of the threat. Cars were parked single file, lining the curb. Sandra and I walked toward hers. Perhaps I was trying to make sense of the press conference; perhaps I was still adjusting to the bright sunlight. Anyway, we were a quarter of the way down the block and we never saw what was coming. I would describe the color as tan, or auburn. It was definitely in the brown family of color. It appeared to be an older model car. One I didn't recognize as it was racing right towards Sandra and me. Quickly leaning to my right, I pushed her in between two parked cars.

My shoulder hit the pavement and pain raced down my right arm. Sandra was face down as I heard the hiss of the racing vehicle go past. Getting to my knees, I poked my head out from one of the vehicles that was safeguarding us. The car had stopped. Maybe forty-feet away, it was turning around clumsily. If I had any doubt about the near miss being deliberate, the doubt was gone. The license plate of the car was obstructed. The windows looked blacker than ink, and the engine was revving to take another pass at Sandra and yours truly, who remained sandwiched between the two parked vehicles.

I did not know what to expect. I wasn't venturing back into the street. Was this person going to jump out and abduct us? Feeling a hand on my arm, I realized Sandra was pulling me in the direction of the sidewalk. We managed to get safely behind a parked car and watched as the tan colored vehicle sped by, propelling loose gravel in our direction. Thanks to the dark windows, we caught not even a glimpse of the driver, but we both knew *who* it was.

"That, my friend, was a *warning*," Sandra said icily.

CHAPTER 14

"DELIBERATE," I SHOUTED, MY voice filling the loft.

Livingston was sitting right where we had left him on the sofa. The appearance of the place hadn't changed at all. He looked remotely interested as I filled him in on the actions of the tan colored car.

"It has to be him," I continued in a demanding tone, completely displaying my fear coupled with my desire for answers. "Was he outside Town Hall today, maybe checking up on us?"

His head inclined slightly as he replied, "Perhaps he was inside attending the meeting."

Sandra and I looked at each other as the words left me a bit spooked. I hadn't even considered it. Who would have known him amongst all those people?

"What did you find out?"

Looking at Sandra, the look on her face told me it was my turn to answer his questions. "I don't know. The police seemed to be pacifying every one. Promising the community they are safe."

He stood up and asked, "Anything else?"

"Lots of pressure from residents. The FBI, as you said earlier, has joined the manhunt."

He walked to the rear of the loft. Sandra looked empty, as if she didn't have much to add. It seemed the stress was draining all of us.

I continued, "It didn't seem like the police had much data. At least none that they could reveal. I don't know, maybe you should have gone yourself. You're so good at looking at things sideways, studying folks, and reading between the lines."

He walked back to the sofa. Over the arm of it he laid a gray overcoat which looked familiar. On top of it he placed a black hat and on top of that a pair of spectacles. Placing a walking stick on the sofa, he looked at me with a sly, knowing smile and I jumped back.

"What the..."

"No way," Sandra came to life.

Both of us stared at him for a couple of seconds, speechless. Now I wanted to know why he was disguised as an old man at Town Hall today. So I asked.

"We're at a disadvantage. This individual knows who we are, but we don't know who he is. This served three purposes," Matthew said, pointing down at his disguise. "I got to look around. A person playing the game he is playing just might turn up at something like this. It would enable him to witness first-hand the panic and concern he has caused."

"Why do that," Sandra asked.

"A carpenter builds and can admire his work. A painter paints and can enjoy what he has created. Being there today would be like seeing his finished product. An entire meeting with law enforcement officials. A town on high alert all because of him. Moreover, it is his art that is being appreciated."

I was impressed. Matthew seemed to be a step ahead of this guy, yet we still hadn't seen him.

Sandra called out, "You said there were three purposes. What's the second and third?"

"The second purpose was that I wanted to ask that question about the military records. I wanted to see if the police were still pursuing that. Apparently they are."

"Which means," I asked, a blank look on my face, which reflected to a certain extent my state of mind.

Looking at Sandra first, then me, he answered, "We must double our efforts because of their dumb decisions."

Overwhelmed was the best description. It was all one big shock for me. The realization of the extent of the danger at hand was causing a bit of distress for me. I noticed Sandra staring at Matt's hands.

He noticed also and commented, "Fake skin sleeves. I was wearing them on my hands. I discarded them once I finished. My face was a combination of makeup applications. I knew the police would not recognize me. More importantly, our shooter would not recognize me."

Sandra's head was shaking in disbelief.

"What now," I pressed.

I never saw him more serious since I've known him. His voice reflected that seriousness.

"I think the police are hoping he will strike again and perhaps they can gather some clues as a result. That was how I interpeted their speech today. If that is the case, someone has to be a victim. In order to do that, we have to identify this guy quickly!"

He made a vague gesture with his hand, dismissing his surroundings.

"My gunpowder theory was a bust, but not fruitless. The powder contained tryptamine. It's a fact I'll put in my back pocket for now. That leads me to my third purpose of disguising myself today."

He began fiddling with the gray overcoat, the top button to be exact. As his fingers gently twisted the button it became detached from the coat. That was when I noticed the thin wire attached to the button that stretched down the length of the coat. Reaching inside a pocket, he removed a small console that was attached to the wire.

"Let's see if we can get a look at your road raged friend," he said handing me the console. Turning it over, I noticed a small view screen.

"I've read about this. Where did you get it," I asked examing the console and the wire.

"It's a buttonhole camera. It records to a hidden MP4 player.

I figured it would help me in viewing the crowd today. I decided to follow you out when you left since I noticed someone following you."

It was amazing! I fiddled with the buttons on the MP4 player as Sandra and Matt crowded around me. The video was perfect. There we were again, back at Town Hall. This time we could hear the conference, but the images were slow scans of the room in brilliant color. The faces of the crowd were as clear as a recording could be. The questions began as another sweep of the room was taken. Matt had the camera eye in a good position. Near the top of his overcoat, it gave him a good level for capturing faces.

I held the MP4 unit low and the three of us stood close together viewing it. After another question was answered, Matt's voice filled the loft.

"Hold it!"

I hit the pause button on the unit as the screen revealed the image of a strange looking man. I didn't recognize him from this afternoon. He had black curly hair with gray infringing on the edges. His eyes were vacuums peering almost painfully outward. Above them were eyebrows that were completely overgrown. His mouth was firm and ruler straight, supported by a hefty chin. Wearing an old looking jacket and dress slacks, he looked so average. Who would pick this person out of a crowd? Certainly not me.

"*There* is the man who followed you!"

It was surreal. On the small screen, I was watching myself with Sandra leaving Town Hall. The buttonhole camera was following us. You could see from a distance, Sandra and I walking toward the Mustang and the curly haired head peeking from behind parked cars. I could see he had put on sunglasses. Suddenly he dashed quickly out of view. The camera view changed as Matt picked up this man getting into the same tan vehicle that tried to do us in. The car sped away from the camera eye as the video abruptly ended.

"I ran pretty fast for an old man, but regretfully the car got out of sight fast."

Sandra laughed, but I still stared down at the MP4 player. I went to hand it back to him and he shook his head.

"Hang onto it. I need you to print some pictures. I'm interested in the close up of that guy's face. We're going to need it."

Sandra asked, "Any glance at a license plate?"

"Yes, but it was obstructed, purposely no doubt!"

Matt sat on the sofa and rested his elbows on his knees. His fingertips gently touched the sides of his face as he stared straight ahead. Sandra had propped herself up on one of the chairs opposite him. It was as if we were waiting for a clue to drop from the sky. We had the shooter's face, but he was still as anonymous as if we hadn't seen him at all.

The Genius broke the silence.

"Make multiple prints from the image we have of this guy."

"I can do that," I answered, realizing he was talking to me.

"Tomorrow morning we need to meet before school starts. Can you have the copies by then?"

"Of course I can."

"Then go now! I need to think about this."

The silence that clung to the loft remained as Sandra and I made our way to the stairs. I turned for a second to look at him. Remaining on the sofa, a contemplative look occupied his face. It was then that I believe I actually saw a slight smile tugging at his lips.

CHAPTER 15

FRIDAYS OFTEN FILL ME with a sense of relief. That was not the case today. As I approached the back door of Serling High School, I saw Matthew Livingston and Sandra Small waiting there. Reaching into my binder, I pulled out three medium-sized envelopes. Each had five copies of the picture of our suspect. Handing Matt his envelope, he immediately slipped his finger under the seal and opened it. Studying the picture, he was careful to keep it close to him so no one around the back door area would see it.

"Keep a copy of this someplace, like in your binder or whatever. Look at it periodically. Study the description. Find some physical depiction that will force you to remember this person. If you are going home today, I want you to be able to recognize this guy from a block away."

"Okay," Sandra nodded her head in agreement, "Sounds cool."

"What now," I whispered.

He put his envelope away in his small shoulder bag.

"I made a few phone calls last night and was able to ascertain some interesting information."

"Like what?"

"Wilson James McMillan has been in Florida for the last two weeks!"

Sandra and I exchanged glances as a nervous feeling scaled my insides.

"It was him at the baseball field," Sandra pronounced. "What a twisted individual!"

"Playing a dangerous game," Matthew replied. "Let's meet in the auditorium before fifth period."

He walked inside with his bag over his shoulder. Determination seemed to be leading him by the hand. With a little less determination, I collected myself and made my way to class.

By the time fourth period ended, I had absorbed extensive reassurance about our school being free of any exposure to the H1N1 flu. Each period began with literature reminding students to wash their hands, like I don't do that, and other day-to-day efforts. If I had heard anymore, I would have morphed into a germaphobe. Heading into the auditorium there was no piano playing today, nor were there any gymnastics. Only the sound of conversation between Sandra and Matthew, who were sitting in the front row of the empty room.

"I was obsessed with this copycat angle, so much so that I feared I had overlooked some things," Matthew began.

"Like what," I asked.

"The obvious!"

A typical answer that I was getting used to hearing from him. It's the type of answer that not only doesn't answer my question, it leaves me thoroughly confused.

"After school can you pay another visit to the library? I need you to look into their computers again."

I felt the smile cross my face. I guess I enjoyed being good at something. Moreover, I enjoyed being called upon to use these talents.

"I can indeed!"

"Be there at 3:15. I will be joining you!"

Sandra looked at both of us and said, "I finish work at eight, you need me?"

"I'll need both of you. We can meet at the loft after eight."

"That's fine with me," she flashed a quick smile.

The two of them stood and picked up their bags. Heading toward the auditorium door, I heard Matthew's voice from behind me.

"One more thing. Be prepared to do some sneaking around!"

She gave the thumbs up sign with much enthusiasm. I thought I was going to be sick.

Chapter 16

THE SETUP WAS PRETTY much the same as Wednesday night. I arranged my gear on a table in the library and surrounded myself with some props as to not arouse any suspicion. The only difference this time was I had Matthew Livingston sitting next to me.

I'm not sure why I bothered with the props, no one was paying any attention to us.

Since Wednesday, the library still hadn't put a firewall up around their computer system, so infiltration was even easier. Matthew told me to revisit the dates I had last viewed, namely the JFK assasination research from a few weeks ago. From there I searched forward and found nothing more on the topic. Which brought us to Tuesday, as in three days ago. There was a lot of research on an FBI probe from the late 1960's concerning someone called the *Zodiac Killer*.

I looked at Livingston and he nodded his head.

"So he's been back here in this library, how did you know?"

"I didn't. I only knew he was here before. My mistake was limiting our search to just the things you found, namely assasinations. There was more! On these computers he has the capability to scour online news articles, once again without leaving a trail on his home computer. The letters to the newspaper started Tuesday evening. He was here Tuesday morning, boning up on his *Zodiac Killer* style of letter writing."

"Look at this," I said, tilting the laptop toward him. "The original *Zodiac Killer* even had a copycat. There's a link to him. And the copycat was searched here as well."

Searching further I announced, "You are right. He was all over the topic of the *Zodiac's* taunting letters."

It was creepy stuff. Especially, if I was following correctly, the *Zodiac Killer* had never been caught.

Matthew spoke, keeping his voice down, "He's copying the style of the letters. That's all. Concentrate on the newspapers. We need to see exactly what he is looking for."

So I did exactly that. He went through newspaper after newspaper, reading all the news on the Caxton shooting and the threatening letters that followed it. He spent time on articles about how the police planned to apprehend him and the charges he was facing.

"What's the last website he views," Matthew asked.

I went forward just a bit, noting that he was on the computer for a total of thirty-two minutes. His last stop was a ticket ordering site.

"Look at this," I said, again tilting the laptop in his direction. He ordered tickets! I can pull up his personal information!"

"*Shhh,*" Matthew said, getting me to quiet my voice that suddenly got louder. We looked around, but like I said, no one was paying us any attention.

I looked into the ticket ordering form and there it was. I pronounced it slowly, "Irving Masterson. My God, we've been living in mortal fear of a guy named Irving?"

"Perhaps that's why he kills people."

He had a notebook open and was jotting the name down. He asked for an address and I read aloud, "Thirty Seven Stebbins Street."

"Great, five blocks away from me. No wonder he probably had no problem tacking that note onto my garage. And what event does the Zodiac wannabe plan on attending?"

Pausing momentarily, I forced the words out.

"The *Extreme Titans Wrestling Network*, Saturday night at Serling High School."

"Go back. Search anything on *Extreme Titans Wrestling*, anything!"

It didn't take long. The last newspaper Irving had read online before he ordered the tickets was our very own *Village Gate*. Yep the very article he previewed was all about *Extreme Titans* coming to Serling High. In addition, featured in a photograph was Senator Hildebrand, Caxton's opponent, who spoke about the popularity of the event and how he would be attending with his twelve-year-old son on Saturday.

I noticed Matthew reading along with me. I backed up in my chair and gazed at him. His eyes remained on the laptop screen for another minute then he looked up at me and spoke.

"Yes, he plans on killing him Saturday."

CHAPTER 17

I COPIED THE NUMBER down from one of those crime stopper posters. It was Detective Withers who answered the phone. After a boatload of complaints, he agreed to meet us. I suggested outside the precinct, so that was where it took place at 8:30 on Friday evening. Sandra was with us and after we filled her in on our discovery, she drove the Genius and me over there. I had a photograph of Irving Masterson concealed in an envelope with his name and address written on the back of it. Leaving the bag with my laptop in the car, I got out and waited with the others.

Based on the brief phone conversation, I wasn't thrilled about dealing with Withers, but Matthew had suggested it. If we turned over the information the police could snatch this guy up before he got near Senator Hildebrand tomorrow night. Besides, Matthew claimed the information was just an indication of a strong possibility. It was a significant lead the police could follow up on and actually do something about.

Withers stepped out of the stationhouse and looked around for a minute until he spotted us. Sandra was leaning against her car with her arms crossed. The black leather jacket and black jeans she wore made her almost invisible in the evening darkness. Matthew was close by. As for me, well I was designated as the talker on this one.

He stood a few feet in front of me with with his hands at his sides.

He was not wearing his suit jacket. On his right hip was a holster with what appeared to be an automatic weapon in it. Something was clutched in his hand, but I couldn't make out what it was.

"Yes," he demanded, in place of a greeting.

I was even less thrilled now. The envelope was in my hands as I conjured up the words.

"We have some information on someone who could possibly be the Caxton shooter."

I remembered what Matthew told me when we had decided to inform the police. We didn't have to reveal anything else. The hacking, the discovery by Singleton Field, or the letter we had received. I had an excuse if he questioned me. Turns out I didn't need it.

"Is that what you made me come down here for," he snarled. He didn't even look at the envelope I was extending to him. The aroma of arrogance could have stripped the paint off of Sandra's car.

"For your information, this investigation is just about wrapped up. We explored our own leads and you can read all about it this weekend in the newspaper."

"Shooter in custody," Matthew asked.

"None of your business," he replied, his arms now folded across his chest.

"How close is just about wrapped up," Matthew asked firmly repeating Wither's own words.

"So close that we no longer need this," he replied roughly thrusting the camera he took from me on Monday into my hand. "And if I find you're interfering in a police investigation, I'll arrest you for obstruction of govermental administration!"

Matt seemed unphased, but I was floored. He wanted nothing from us and clearly wanted nothing to even do with this. It was crazy! He turned around and headed back into the precinct. I turned and looked at my friends.

"What do we do?"

Matthew answered me, "If we do nothing, this time tomorrow there could be another victim."

Sandra took her keys out of her jacket pocket and started filtering them through her fingers as she commented, "We need a plan."

We got in the car and drove.

Sandra had put some distance between the precinct and us. Parking on a quiet street in town, she turned to face Matthew who was sitting in the passenger's seat.

"Do you have it," she asked him.

I didn't know what she was talking about. Perhaps they had engaged in a conversation before I arrived in the auditorium this morning.

"I received it before I met Dennis at the library."

I was clueless. Whatever they were talking about, Matthew removed from his inside jacket pocket something so small it was concealed in his hand. Reaching into the back where I was seated he handed me a small square object.

My eyes grew large and my mouth opened as I exclaimed, "Whoa!"

I recognized it instantly. It was a GPS tracking device. I knew everything about them, but never actually saw one up close.

"Mr. Masterson definitely knows who we are, so we can't get too close to him. But, there's nothing stopping us from knowing where he is, provided he drives."

Sandra's lips surrendered into a sympathetic smile as she saw the overwhelmed look upon my face. I had spent hours on tech web sites reading about this unit and here I had one in my hand. Then, as usual, came the stunning realization that this was going to be accompanied by some sort of dangerous task.

Matthew looked at me and added, "We have a month's worth of free service and the battery is charged for five days of continual use."

My voice was racing with excitement.

"All I have to do is download the software and I can follow it from my laptop, my cellphone, and…"

"First things first," Sandra chimed in, "we've got to get it into Masterson's car."

"That's going to require a little stealth mode," Matthew answered her. "I was kind of counting on you for that."

Sandra pulled out her knit cap and laid it on top of her thigh. On top of that, she placed a pair of black leather gloves and a small leather case which she opened to reveal some tiny flat looking tools. Slapping her hand down on top of them, she pronounced, "Done!"

"Before we roll," I said, "we are going to need to activate this unit." I pulled my laptop out of its protective bag and turned it on.

Matthew handed me a disc that contained the program for the tracking unit.

After I entered the serial number of the device, my laptop downloaded all of the applications. We were set. Now for the hard part.

According to Matthew's profiling of Irving Masterson, he didn't have much of a night life. With that in mind we decided to head toward Stebbins Street to see if we could spot the vehicle that tried to turn Sandra and I into road kill yesterday.

"We have to maintain some distance," Matthew said as the vehicle passed block after block of tree lined streets. "If he's around and spots this vehicle, he will probably recognize it from Wednesday when you rescued us."

She acknowledged his insight by bouncing her right fist off the steering wheel.

The Genius continued, "Its dark. We can use that to our advantage. First, however, we need to locate the vehicle, assuming he parks it near his house. Sandra is going to plant the tracking unit. We can't risk burning her by having her locate the car and then planting the device in it. When we get near Stebbins Street, let me out. I got a good look at the vehicle on the video I took. I can recognize it."

Sandra gave him the make and model, in case he didn't already know.

"I have that overcoat and hat from the other day. It should be enough. I will walk northbound on Stebbins Street. I'll examine the block, especially Masterson's house. I need the two of you to park a block away, but in the direction I'm walking. If it's there, we'll disguise Dennis and send him down the block a little bit in front of you, on the opposite side of the street. Once you see Sandra getting close to wherever the car is, you stop and pretend you are getting a call on your cellphone. Do whatever you have to, but give the appearance of someone who can't walk and talk on the phone. Pace back and forth if you have to. If anyone is out on the block create a diversion for Sandra. Keep an eye out! If you encounter trouble, alert her on her cell phone."

"Okay," I began, "before we get to the plan, did you just say 'we'll disguise Dennis'?"

Sandra had stopped the car and got out. I heard the trunk of the car being opened. In a moment, she reached in the back seat and something was deposited in my lap.

"Nice," I shouted unfolding the old leather jacket Sandra had loaned me once before. It was a battle-worn looking piece of material that somehow managed to give me a shot of confidence. The jacket was accompanied by a black knit cap, similar to Sandra's.

"This should be good," Matthew exclaimed, referring to our position.

"Give us three minutes to set up on the other end," Sandra said. "I left the trunk open so you can grab your things."

He exited. Shortly after, I saw him wearing the gray overcoat and black hat. Sandra drove off, certain not to drive down Stebbins Street where we could be spotted. When we reached our destination, which was two blocks north of Masterson's house, she parked and we waited.

Roughly ten minutes later, Livingston was approaching Sandra's car. He climbed in the back as I had taken his place in the passenger's seat.

"I thought at first it wasn't there, but it is. The car is up the driveway, in the rear of the house. The block is pretty quiet, just one man walking a dog. There are no exterior house lights burning, that's why I had trouble spotting the vehicle."

"Then, I'm going straight up the driveway," Sandra stated.

She tucked her red hair under the black knit cap. Putting on the gloves she tapped me on the arm and said, "Let's do this." She extended a gloved hand palm up and I placed the GPS tracking unit in it.

I ran through my instructions again. Letting her get about a quarter of a block in front of me, I crossed over to the opposite side of the street. Maybe it was anxiety, but she was really moving. I picked up my pace a little to keep up as we hit the block of 17 Stebbins Street.

Grabbing my cellphone, I stopped and examined it as she turned into the driveway. The dark green house to the left of it looked sinister as the faint night swallowed the dark image of Sandra Small.

I talked into the Blackberry as if I were receiving a call. As I made some small conversation, I looked around. The guy walking his dog was further down the block with his back to me. Another person a few houses away deposited a trash can on the curb and returned to his house, clearly oblivious to my presence. Stebbins Street was very quiet.

A few minutes later Sandra reappeared and I stayed with my phone call. I almost missed her as she exited the driveway and continued in the direction that she was originally walking. I decided to start walking myself. When I hit the corner, I turned right and back tracked on the adjacent street, making my way to the Mustang. When I arrived, Sandra was already there.

Once we were all inside, I needed the details.

Starting the car she said, "That's definitely the car that tried to run us down. An older model with no alarm, so getting inside of it was simple."

"Where did you plant it," I asked nervously.

Driving, she replied, "Inside the fuzzy dice hanging from the rearview mirror, where else?"

"Where," Livingston and I inquired loudly in unison.

"I'm kidding. He has those old vinyl seat covers that zipper shut. I opened one and inserted it there."

Sandra hung a turn as the car sped up. She seemed to have a destination in mind.

Matthew said, "We need to look at this tracking program and make sure everything is working."

That meant we were headed to the loft.

CHAPTER 18

LIVINGSTON AND I WERE seated on the tired sofa viewing the screen on my laptop. It was displaying a map of our neighborhood. A blinking icon was displayed on Stebbins Street.

"I was reading about a feature this unit has," I began. "It's called the *Fence*. It lets you create boundary lines, or a so-called fence. If the vehicle you're tracking crosses this fence, the unit immediately notifies you."

He was adamant as he said, "OK, set up a boundary around the school. Go one block away in each direction. If Masterson drives tomorrow night, he is sure to find parking within a block of the school area. This will alert us to his arrival!"

"Done," I said as I set up the boundaries and programmed the *Fence* to notify me via my cell phone.

Sandra was sitting backwards on a folding chair as she asked, "How do we roll tomorrow?"

Matthew stood up and asked, "Did you take care of that matter we spoke about?"

I thought he was talking to me as I looked blankly at him.

It was Sandra who answered, "Oh, yes I did. I almost forgot about that." She was fishing through her jacket pockets when she pulled out a laminated item that was attached to a yellow chord. She dropped it on the wheel top as I gave it a closer inspection.

"Wow," I gasped. "First the GPS tracker, now this. It must be Christmas and someone forgot to tell me."

I held it in my hands. Looking through the plastic laminate I saw the *Extreme Titans Wrestling* logo. Flipping it over it read *ALL ACCESS/PRESS*.

Matthew looked down at me and said, "This gets you in and around tomorrow night before the general public."

"How'd you get this?"

Sandra replied, "Our school newspaper's senior editor, Stephen Ross, owes me big time. I helped him pass auto mechanics class. He's working on his GPA in hopes of a scholarship. If not for me, he'd be out of luck. Stephen cleared it with Mr. C and *you* are the replacement."

"Sweet!"

Sitting next to me again, Matthew commanded our attention. His hands became clenched balls of intensity as he spoke.

"Once again, I can not say it enough. Study that picture of Masterson! Tomorrow's event is going to be packed. The better we know this person's description, the better chance we have of spotting him."

He was directing the next part to me.

"Sandra and I bought tickets; we will be in the area, but obviously not before you. Since you programmed the *Fence*, you will be alerted when our friend is near. Whatever this guy is planning he will probably keep his weapon close by, if not on him. If we can identify him and locate the weapon, we will simply call the police. The main thing is that no one gets shot, namely Senator Hildebrand."

"Communication," I asked.

"You have each other's cellphone numbers. I will carry one as well, so program the number."

Sandra and I retrieved our phones and entered the ten numbers he recited. Having done that I pocketed mine and returned my attention to Mr. Livingston.

He slowly raised himself up from the couch and walked behind Sandra. His right hand aggressively stroked his chin.

"If he uses the same weapon, chances are it could be disassembled. Perhaps in a bag, perhaps. Who knows, he may just be using a handgun. I'm not sure. But these are things we need to be on the lookout for."

The press pass was hanging from my neck. My fingers were grasping the edges of it as I ran through the gameplan in my head. It seemed very one dimensional, with little chance for mistakes. Somehow I doubted it would work out that way.

Sandra turned her head and focused on Livingston who was still standing behind her. "Correct me if I'm wrong," she began, "Masterson's whole point is to not get caught, right? That is what all his teasing letters were about. So can we expect him to be in hiding when he attempts to pick off the Senator?"

"We are dealing with a lunatic," he said with a drop of doubt in his voice. "To people who know him it's conceivable that he's viewed as an odd man who probably lives in his mother's basement and never adjusted to society. The fact is, he was very sucessful in his actions. He didn't get caught. He probably feels his crimes are justified, therefore I expect the game is still the same. He plans on getting away with it. Probably already planning his next batch of letters to scare everyone with. Sorry to disappoint him, but *I'm* not scared!"

The vacuum of silence in the loft may have swallowed his words, but the message lingered. It was admirable. Then I thought of Masterson and only one word came to mind.

"Freaky," I commented. "This guy is just plain freaky. I'm worried."

"Don't put yourself at such a disadvantage Dennis. After all, the tables are turned slightly in our favor."

I scratched my modestly gelled hair and asked, "How so?"

"Correct me if I'm wrong but, with our GPS tracking device in place, Mr. Masterson has now become the target."

My mouth turned upright as a combined sense of relief and exhilaration took hold of me. Sandra was smiling as well.

"Game on," she shouted as if it was a battle cry.

However Matthew did it, he invigorated us. It wasn't that skeptical feeling hanging over me for once. I stood as tall as I could.

"I will contact both of you tomorrow," he said reverting to his solemn tone of voice. "Again, look at that photo, learn it!"

With those instructions, we left.

Chapter 19

Saturday evening arrived. Matthew had called me before I left for Serling High School. He said one news station was reporting that the police were questioning a suspect in regard to Caxton's murder. Maybe that was why Detective Withers wasn't interested in our information. Matthew assured me they were wrong.

As I gazed around the empty gymnasium I thought about where I would situate myself if I were a sniper. The gym had been expanded to accommodate its maximum capacity, so there was that much more room to hide. The basketball hoops were retracted and the accordian bleachers were stretched out as far as possible. Aisles of chairs filled out the floor area.

This set-up was on all four sides surrounding the ring. A few men, sporting blue shirts that read *EXTREME* in capital, bold yellow letters across the back were hard at work inside of it. They were installing the corner posts, which supported the ropes. On the ring apron was a banner displaying the *Extreme Titans* logo.

I double checked my cell phone to make sure it was charged. It was fine. Patting my hip pocket, I felt the backup battery. Inside my denim jacket, I reassured myself by feeling for my ear piece. My notebook was available as was the digital camera I brought along for pictures. I was set. I realized the three of us would be seperated most of the night. Communication was critical for our own safety as well as the success of Livingston's plan. It was going to get loud tonight, so I felt text messaging was the best way to go.

Seeing that the ring construction was finished, I walked around a bit, observing all that was involved with the Extreme operation. It was interesting. Vendors with their goods were stretched across the hallway outside the gym. Women and men were stocking supplies and counting money, while attendants were readying their scanner guns in anticipation of the ticket holders who would be arriving shortly.

Also stretching down the hall was the aroma of hot dogs boiling and sauerkraut in a steam pan. My stomach took notice as I hadn't eaten much today. But I had other things to keep myself occupied with. I had a story to write that I knew was important. I was covering a sports entertainment event. That was also important. Then there was our little side purpose. The one where according to Matthew Livingston and his science of deduction, Senator Hildebrand was a dead man walking! Not good, but certainly relevent, especially to the Senator.

Back in the gym, a big black curtain had been hung like a veil between two sections of bleachers. It was situated behind them, I guessed, to hide the wrestlers before they were announced. Feeling for the opening in the veil, I flapped it aside to reveal the office utilized by our gym teachers. I entered.

It looked completely different. A large group of people were inside of it and no one noticed me enter. It was a harsh realization that in sixteen years on this planet, not a lot of people noticed me. Well tonight I would use that to my advantage. Leaning against the wall with my notebook out and press pass displayed, I observed the strange scene in front of me.

About twenty muscular men were parading around in tights or athletic trunks, as well as boots. Some displayed flashy robes and others disguised themselves in face paint. And then there was one fellow who was wearing, I kid you not, a robot costume. I think he noticed me staring at him adjusting his mask, so I decided to look occupied. I took out the digital camera and started playing with it. Moving like he was made out of metal, he turned to face me.

"No pictures without the mask on," he said in a corny mechanical voice.

"No problem," I said, waving my hand in a sign of assurance.

As we had this exchange, another wrestler was practicing flips. He would run toward the wall and kick off it, propelling his body into a somersault.

Next to a large coffee urn sat two wrestlers I immediately recognized. They were chatting as they examined a tray of doughnuts positioned on top of a desk.

I was confused. I grabbed an event program that was on the same desk. Yep, I was right. They were squaring off against each other in the main event. Talk about scripted outcomes.

Something else the fans never see was spread about the room. Doctors. I counted three guys in white coats that read *State Athletic Commission* across the left front. Sliding stethoscopes around wrestler's chests, they appeared more mechanical than the guy in the robot suit.

Different grapplers were getting a handful of examinations. I found it interesting that these guys ran wild in the ring, but in reality they didn't run anywhere unless a doctor cleared them.

"Hey buddy," a colorful looking guy called to me. He wore lime green tights with yellow boots that matched his long hair. He was seated with a doctor in front of him, taking his blood pressure.

"You doin' a story on us tonight? I bet for the school newspaper, right?"

I secured the camera around my neck and replied, "That's correct." I felt comfortable so I sat close to him and flipped to a clean page in my notebook. Looking at him close up, I recalled his name.

Hangman Hally Rhodes!

I didn't recognize him at first because on TV he was always screaming, but presently he seemed quite sedate.

"Well get ready," the screaming began, but not as overbearing as it was when he appeared in the ring during televised events. "The Hangman will continue down his path of destruction tonight with Oregon Dale being his next victim!"

He yanked his forearm downward in a menacing motion, accenting his statement. I jotted it down in my notebook and couldn't help but notice his statement read like one of Masterson's threats. Weird!

"Blood pressure is one ten over seventy," The doctor reported.

"Great," Hally commented. "Time for this."

Reaching under his long hair he retrieved a cigarette that was trapped behind his ear. Lighting it up he opened the office window and exhaled a cloud of smoke into the night.

"Need a picture," a monotone voice interjected.

I looked around and realized it was the doctor who was writing on a chart.

"Sure. Thanks," I replied handing him the camera.

Quickly disgarding the cigarette, Hally threw his arm around me and posed. A bright flash ignited and the doctor handed me back the camera.

A middle-aged guy with brown curly hair walked by us and Hally said to me, "See this guy here." His thumb jerked in the direction of the man. "He's stealing money tonight."

Hally's statement was accompanied by a hearty laugh as I quickly realized he was breaking the guy's chops.

"Seriously," he continued, "I want you to meet Ray. When I hang up the wrestling tights, I want Ray's job."

I shook hands with him and inquired, "What do you do Ray?"

He seemed friendly enough as he replied, "I'm working the spotlight tonight."

"Stealing money," Hally joked. "Seriously, you have to shine the thing when people walk down the aisle. Damn, I want that job. I take a beating in the ring and he shines a light, what am I doing wrong?"

Both of them laughed together as strange noises consumed the office space. Doctors were dryly giving instructions to the athletes. The occassional slapping sound could be heard as I realized the somersault artist was actually barefoot. There was also a groan of disappointment as the robot realized he had to take off his costume to get his chest examined. Then I heard the strangest noise of all. It was like a strong vibration was crushing gravel.

"That you kid," Hally asked me, hearing it also.

Reaching in my pocket I examined my cell phone. Masterson had arrived!

CHAPTER 20

REMAINING VIRTUALLY UNNOTICED, I stood up quite suddenly. Focused on the energy and excitement of the growing crowd, which could be heard from the office, and the upcoming opportunity to entertain, these people were clearly in show time mode. Now I had to be also. Hally was searching for another cigarette. The doctor, who conducted his examination, had forgotten rubbing alcohol and went to get some. The somersault man stood still for a moment and was adjusting his kneepads.

A tall, lanky fellow entered wearing one of the blue shirts emblazoned with the word *Extreme*. Clutching a clipboard, he glanced around at the performers.

"Listen up," he said loudly, getting everyone's attention. "Let's go over the order of tonight's program."

I stepped around the gathering warriors and headed toward the office door. Once outside, I grabbed my phone and dialed Matthew.

"I just got the alert," I said nervously, "he's in the area."

"I'm inside and so is Sandra," he replied calmly.

"What should we do?"

"I wouldn't mind getting him on the ticket line and getting this over with. The only trouble is I'm on the other side of the gym and if he recognizes you, he'll probably bolt."

Telling him to hold the line, I connected my earpiece so I could keep my hands free. Stepping into the hall, where the vendors stood earlier, I turned left. Walking quickly down the hall, I was met by a rope barrier. The barrier was preventing people who were arriving at the event from utilizing this particular corridor.

"I'm in the hallway outside the gym. I can see the ticket holders entering. You want me to observe from here?"

"Yes, but don't be seen. I'm trying to get closer to your location. Let me call you back."

"I'm fine. Everyone is in a line getting his or her tickets scanned. They're all looking in the opposite direction and I've got a good side view."

Ending our phone call, I waited and waited. I saw profile after profile making their way closer to the gym entrance. The line was moving faster now. It was a cast of characters. Mostly teenagers. They were in groups of three or four and dressed colorfully. I also saw a decent number of adults. Some accompanied younger kids and some who must have been closet wrestling fans.

Then there was Masterson.

He stood dead last in line by himself. A black baseball cap was concealing his hair and forehead. That robust chin was still unmistakable. He wore the same old looking jacket he was wearing at Town Hall. It was easy for me to spot him. After all, I had spent a good part of the afternoon studying his picture. The most important thing I noticed was that his hands were free.

Retreating down the hallway, I called Livingston and gave him the update accompanied by Masterson's description and location. He informed me that he would have to pick him up inside the gym.

The next thing I heard was noise, an announcer's voice. The event was starting. Heading back inside, the lights had dimmed. Ray directed his spotlight as Wildman Jayson bounded through the black curtain. The crowd booed intensely.

Security inspected my press pass and allowed me to walk behind a section of bleachers, getting closer to the main door. I saw no sign of Masterson.

Wildman was now in the ring. I recognized the man announcing, as he had been in the office earlier. His voice was resonating, echoing throughout the gymnasium and infusing the crowd with a genuine sense of anticipation. "Before I announce his opponent, I would like to introduce, sitting at ringside, the man who was instrumental in bringing Extreme Titans here tonight. Please give a round of applause to Senator Hildebrand."

Applause sounded as my blood turned cold. Senator Hildebrand was stepping into the ring. My knees started to weaken as I made a last ditch effort to spot Masterson amongst the crowd of cheering fans.

"*Where are you,*" I pleaded with myself.

Hildebrand received the applause graciously and gave a friendly wave to the crowd. And, that was it. He returned to his seat at ringside.

Nothing happened.

As they announced Wildman Jayson's opponent, I continued to scan the crowd. The black hat was nowhere.

Ray had his spotlight going as someone was running towards the ring, but I couldn't see who. The frenzy of the crowd erupted as Wildman attacked the man before he gained access to the ring. I made a mental note to check the program later to make sure I had the correct names for my story.

An incoming call from Matthew prompted me to make my way to the quiet hallway again. His intensity was at an all time high.

"This guy has been here before. He knows the layout too well."

"I don't follow," I said, a bit confused.

"He knows this whole layout. He slipped by the main door and vanished."

"It's a pretty big crowd, with lots of people standing. You sure we didn't just miss him?"

"Yes. Moreover, if I'm right, which I'm confident I am, he has had prior access to this facility. He could have concealed his weapon…"

There was an interuption in his voice…

"What's wrong," I panicked.

"Concealed," he shouted over some background noise.

I was clueless.

"The letter he wrote to the paper, he spoke of concealing himself in time. He's dropping clues. Where is concealed time?"

"I haven't the…"

"The scoreboard clock, for the basketball games!"

I went silent and thought about it. The scoreboard clock. I didn't play basketball well, but I had worked the clock a few times. You had to walk inside the clock itself to fire up the lights. There was room inside the inner workings of the clock for two or three people.

"Where are you?"

I gave him my location and realized he wouldn't be allowed access. He hung up before I could tell him. Standing in the hall waiting, I noticed a security person moving the barrier. Sandra, with her hand wrapped in a bandage, was being accompanied by one of the State Athletic Commission doctors, the one who took my picture. He was carrying a small black bag.

I wondered if she was in a brawl or something. Sandra never got hurt, even with all the extracurrilur activities she did. Maybe an accident?

"What happened," I asked.

"Nothing," she whispered in my direction.

I looked at the doctor and he spoke. No way! It was him all along. He had been with me the whole time in the office. The hair was colored blond, the nose was completely different, and the eyebrows had been altered. It was Livingston! There wasn't time to ask him any questions.

"How do we get to that balcony where the scoreboard clock is located?"

I knew this. The clock was on a balcony overlooking the gym, but you could only access it from the second floor.

"Upstairs," I replied pointing up.

"Lead the way," he ordered.

I started to walk, but Sandra grabbed my arm.

"Were you really hugging one of the wrestlers?"

"No," I fired in defense.

Up one flight of stairs we found the second floor and it was dimly lit. The pale blue door in the middle of the hall was what we wanted. Before I could open it Matthew tapped me on my shoulder.

"When was the last time Serling had a home basketball game?"

I remembered Shelley Coverdale reported on the last home game for the school paper's recent issue.

"Two weeks," I stated.

"Does the clock get used for any other event?"

"No, just basketball."

He looked at Sandra and I and nodded his head, "Oh yeah, he's in there. He has concealed himself in that gigantic clock. He probably has his weapon stashed in there as well."

Sandra was unravelling the bandage from her hand and tugged at both ends of it like she was ready to strangle someone. She added, "If he knew the schedule he could have hid it in there in advance."

"Let me see your camera," Matthew asked.

I handed it over to him. Examining it briefly he asked, "Did you change any settings since I took your picture earlier?"

"No," I replied, wondering what he was getting at.

"Good," he said satisfied. Reaching for the door knob he commented, "Try not to get shot in here."

Turning the knob slowly, the door began to budge. Matthew stepped inside as the noise of the crowd below got louder. It was dark on the balcony, darker than it should have been. The width of the whole terrace was about thirty feet. At the very edge of it was the ominious scoreboard clock. It was bolted to the floor and stood about six feet high. The lights on the front of it were raised and faced the gymnasium below when a basketball game was being played. Tonight they were off and to the left of it sat a decent sized spotlight on a rotating mount. A few feet behind the spotlight, on the floor, was Ray unconscious with his hands, feet, and mouth bound.

Matthew lifted the camera and extended it out to the right of the scoreboard. It was then that I noticed the dark figure huddled between the edge of the scoreboard and the wall.

"Get ready Sandra," he called out as she rummaged through the black bag.

Running closer, Livingston ignited the flash on the camera and it illuminated the whole veranda. He flattened his back against the scoreboard clock. Turning quickly was Masterson. The vacuum like eyes were fixed right on me and fixed right in his hands was a shotgun.

Sandra lunged out with something in her right hand. A beam of light projected as I realized she was holding a large metal flashlight.

I had tunnel vision. Even in this dark setting, my eyes locked on Masterson who was recoiling in obvious discomfort. His hands clutched the gun by the long barrel and he swung the butt of it wildly. It connected with Sandra's flashlight and knocked it to the floor. Masterson's eyes were widening as he adjusted his grip properly on the gun. I stood frozen, my feet feeling like bricks of clay. I had to drop down and shield myself somehow. Sandra was down on one knee looking like the blow caught part of her hand. On my left by the scoreboard, I noticed Livingston was gone. Masterson was raising the weapon up to eye level when the balcony became ablaze with blinding brilliance.

Diving to the floor, there was very little cover and I found myself next to Ray who was stirring. Looking up, Livingston had the spotlight pinned on Masterson in a hot white assault. The gun hit the floor as he crashed to his knees clutching his eyes, which were clearly burning from the intensity of the light.

There was a flurry of motion in the close quarters that surrounded us. Sandra reclaimed her large flashlight and clubbed the kneeling figure on the side of his head, causing much pain. Matthew refused to release the spotlight as Masterson's body jerked upward and back against the wall. He had abandoned the weapon and was rolling along the wall in obvious distress.

"He has photophobia," Matthew said smiling at me.

A ringing noise sounded as I took notice of another door in the balcony area. FIRE DOOR was written across it. Masterson had tumbled into the aperture and was clearly seeking to make an escape.

After turning off the powerful spotlight, Matthew began attempts to release whatever was binding Ray's mouth.

"We'll get you free in a minute," he instructed him, "we have to catch that maniac first."

"No argument here," Ray responded gratefully.

Sandra had caught the door before it closed. The ringing continued, but hardly loud enough to cause a disturbance past the balcony area. Matthew and I fell in behind her and pursued Masterson who was descending the staircase rampantly, while grappling for the bannister.

He had reached the first floor landing as Sandra gained on him. He was still in agony as I realized that photophobia was a sensitivity to light disorder. I thought about the intensity of that spotlight. Ouch!

Sandra had grabbed him and forced him into the pushbar on the door on the landing. I had never used this staircase before and when Masterson's body forced open the door I could tell we were in the anteroom, behind the black curtain next to the gym office.

Masterson was face down on the floor and Sandra was holding him there, driving a knee into his back. Matthew and I stood behind her. A security person was stationed by the door, which led to the hallway I had been using earlier. He ran over with a two-way radio in his hand.

"This guy was in the balcony with a shotgun, pointing it into the crowd."

The guard must have noticed the anxiety in my voice as he

quickly called for back-up over his radio. Leaning over to assist Sandra, he looked at Masterson who was in bad shape.

"The weapon is still up there and the spotlight operator is tied up," I added.

"Get someone up to the second floor balcony," he shouted into the radio. He took control of Masterson who suddenly became quite compliant.

Matthew tugged on my jacket sleeve and I followed him into the hallway. Sandra relinquished her hold of Masterson to the security guard and joined us in the open hallway.

I still didn't recognize him in the disguise as he spoke.

"Stay here. Cover your story. When the police arrive tell them you went up to interview the spotlight operator or something along those lines and spotted Masterson. Not a word about the investigation to anyone. I'll call Withers in a half an hour and suggest a connection between this incident and the Caxton killing."

"Okay," I said confidently. "I can do that."

"We're leaving before any attention gets drawn to us."

"I understand."

"Besides," Sandra chimed in, "we pulled a favor to get that Athletic Commission's doctor's coat and I need to return it."

Perhaps it was the adrenaline rush I had just experienced on the balcony, but her words didn't phase me. I didn't even want to know how they pulled it off.

"What street did Masterson park on," he asked me.

Looking at the GPS application on my cellphone I replied, "Sawyer."

"Good. I need that tracking unit back."

CHAPTER 21

UNIFORMED POLICE OFFICERS HAD arrived. They had Irving Masterson in custody. I explained that I wanted to get a bird's eye view of the event to take pictures for my story when I saw Masterson with the shotgun and he fled downstairs. They had Masterson, the weapon, and were getting a story from Ray who was expounding upon the fact that he was struck from behind with a blunt instrument. The police were grateful that I decided to go up to the balcony at just that time.

I covered my story, taking notes on all the matches that took place. Deep down, however, I was wondering if the main story would be perhaps the capture of Irving Masterson.

Ray had thanked me considerably. He didn't ask any questions. He was just relieved that we had discovered him. Besides, the real doctor never showed himself, so as far as he was concerned that was who was up in the balcony, not Matthew Livingston.

The crowd was roaring as the event progressed. They were oblivious to all the drama. I made my way back into the gym office and *The Hangman* was there.

Again he threw his arm around me and I looked around to make sure Sandra was really gone.

"Hey buddy," he said looking down at me. "Ray told me what you did. That was pretty brave. The Hangman wants to thank you personally. As crazy as this business is, I couldn't imagine working an event without Ray. Even if he is stealing money."

We laughed.

Sunday afternoon when I entered the loft little had changed, physically. Nevertheless, in reality, a lot had changed as a great weight had been lifted from my shoulders. Namely, a target was removed from my body. And speaking of changes, his hair was dark again and I had no trouble recognizing Matthew Livingston, who was sitting on the sofa. In the center of the wheeltop was today's newspaper.

Sitting in one of the folding chairs I grabbed the paper and opened it. I needed to remind myself that it was all over. I flipped to the article that said Masterson was in custody and being questioned about the Caxton murder. I exhaled.

"Why do I sense you're about to ask me a bunch of questions," he commented as I returned the paper to its resting place.

"*Photophobia*?"

"An intolerance to light," he replied looking past me.

"And we know this how?"

"Three things. When I observed him at Town Hall he put sunglasses on as he departed."

"So did half the audience. Do you remember how bright it was that afternoon?"

"He was in a horrible rush to put them on and the frequency of his blinking was tremendous. Also the lenses were specially tinted. Rose colored. Remember the powder I found and tested? I identified trace amounts of tryptamine, the foundation for a compound common in migrane medication. Migranes are a common ailment of photophobia. The third indication was when Sandra got into Masterson's car to plant the tracking unit. She recognized something odd about the windows. I went and spoke to an optomologist who I know and he confirmed my suspicions. He informed me that someone who suffers from photophobia may have tinted car windows to decrease sensitivity to light."

I went to scratch my head and remembered I had recently styled it. I resigned myself to the fact that I would never know how his mind worked or why my hair resisted any attempts on my part to make it look right.

He stood up and walked around the sofa. Looking into the rear of the loft he said, "A news report on the radio sheds little light on the situation. They do indicate that Senator Hildebrand was indeed a target. Masterson's motives are being described as intermittent insanity."

I couldn't put my finger on it, but something was troubling him. We spoke for a few more minutes and then I told him I would see him at school tomorrow. Leaving the loft, the walk home seemed longer than usual.

Monday morning I arrived at school and walked towards the back entrance. Sandra was getting out of her car. She wasn't wearing the leather jacket, but might have wished she was. The wind was kicking up a bit of a chill.

Securing a couple of books under her right arm she asked, "How are you doing?"

"Pretty good. I wrote two stories based on the events of Saturday evening. One covers the wrestling matches, the other covers Masterson's side show. We'll see which one Mr. C wants to run in the paper."

Her head kicked to the left as she dodged some debris that was blowing in the damp air. The gray morning was encroaching. Getting a better grip on her books she said, "That was a close call up there in that balcony."

I nodded my head in agreement. I suddenly felt exhausted as my memory began to replay the events. Looking toward the back door, I noticed Matthew Livingston approaching us. I felt a raindrop as I turned to face him.

Cracking a smile I said, "We did it, we pulled it off. I feel pretty good. A little aged from fear but overall…"

"Masterson is dead!"

His words hit me right in the guts. His face was like granite as he stared at us. I wasn't sure if he wanted a comment, so I tried to think one up, but was really too shocked to think of anything sensible at the moment.

"What happened," Sandra asked eyes wide.

"Last night, after another round of police interrogation, he somehow managed to get his hands on a cyanide capsule. No explanations yet."

I wasn't sure why he seemed so irritated, even angry. As far as I was concerned it was one less homicidal maniac in the world. I looked at Sandra and she wasn't saying anything. The wind was brushing the red hair that hung from the knit cap on her head. She glanced up as a few drops of rain landed on her.

Shrugging my shoulders I said, "Looks like he really won't be bothering us anymore. He's gone."

"And so is his information. I refuse to believe this was an isolated incident. The methodical plotting suggests so much more. So much more that we may never know. He took his information with him. One week ago this ordeal began. We may have saved a man's life, but we are none the wiser to a possible motive. We learned nothing!"

He turned and headed for the door. Sandra and I exchanged one more glance with expressionless faces. Rain began to fall heavily as I watched him walk.